Follow Andrina Adamo's dancing career through these new editions of the Drina ballet books.

The Drina books:

Drina Dances
in Italy

by

Jean Estoril

SIMON & SCHUSTER
YOUNG BOOKS

Cover artwork by Kevin Jones
Cover design by Terence Kingston
Illustrations by Jenny Sanders

First published in Great Britain by Hodder & Stoughton Ltd
Second edition published in Great Britain by MacDonald & Co
(Publishers) Ltd

This edition published in 1992 by
Simon & Schuster Young Books
Campus 400
Maylands Avenue
Hemel Hempstead HP2 7EZ

Printed and bound at Cox & Wyman Ltd, Reading, Berkshire,
England

British Library Cataloguing in Publication Data available

ISBN: 0-7500-1263-3

CONTENTS

BOOK ONE
Ballet in London

1

Almost a new Girl

Drina was dreaming that she was Little Clara in the ballet *Casse Noisette*. It was an extraordinarily vivid dream, for she could smell the cool, woody smell of the stage and even feel the draught blowing from the wings. She was sitting on the stage in her nightgown, watching the Nutcracker Prince dancing with the Snow Queen and the only peculiar thing about it was that the Snow Queen was in practice costume. This, Drina was sure, was very odd indeed, because it was a real performance. Beyond the orchestra pit she could see the darkened auditorium in which seemed to float hundreds of pale faces.

Quickly the scene changed and she was in the Kingdom of Sweets. Only she was not sitting watching as Little Clara should have done, but was dancing more and more wildly as all the familiar characters looked on. Then suddenly the Sugar Plum Fairy, who looked very like Miss Volonaise from the Dominick Ballet School, was standing in front of her, crying in a loud voice:

"Stop at once, Drina Adams! You're stealing the show. Don't you know that you're not even in the Company?"

At that awful moment the dream faded and Drina found herself in her own bed in the dark, shivering with cold because the bedclothes had almost slipped to the floor. She tugged them back into position and, looking at the illuminated dial of her watch, found that it was seven o'clock. Seven o'clock in the morning that she was to go back to the Dominick School after nearly a year's absence at the residential school in Buckinghamshire!

It was just as well that she was awake early, Drina thought, as she began to get warm again. It would give her time to think about things. There had been little enough chance during the Christmas holidays, especially as her friend Jenny Pilgrim had been staying at the flat in Westminster until the previous day.

The holidays had been wonderful. First Christmas at a hotel with her grandparents, who had so recently returned from Australia, then settling down in the flat, meeting Jenny, going to theatres and concerts.

But now the holidays were over and that very morning – such a cold morning it seemed, too – she was to go back to the Dominick School in Red Lion Square.

The strange thing was that, instead of being happy and excited, Drina was conscious of distinct uneasiness, a slight reluctance to face the day.

"I hated leaving the Dominick," she thought. "And I hated Chalk Green Manor when I first went there last March. I ought to be glad to be back in London – I am *really*. But I do dread this term a bit. I suppose it's partly because Rose will still be going to Chalk Green and I shall be almost a new girl at the Dominick."

Rose Conway, apart from Jenny who lived in Willerbury, a Warwickshire town, was Drina's best friend, and it was certainly sad to think of Rose returning to Chalk Green while Drina herself crossed Red Lion Square and went up the once so familiar steps of the Dominick School.

Rose had followed Drina to the Chilterns after Easter the previous year, for she had been given a residential scholarship on health grounds. The scholarship would last for another year, at least.

"I shall miss her so dreadfully!" Drina said aloud.

Lying there, she admitted to herself that she would miss much else besides, even though it *was* lovely to be back in London and to have her grandparents home again. She would miss her friends at Chalk Green, the little mongrel dog Petrouchka and, above all, she would miss the Chiltern Hills and the wintry beechwoods.

Last March she had been a town mouse, hating the country and only longing for city streets, but she had learned a great deal since then. Summer in the country had been delightful and autumn had been beautiful, too, with pale, chalky ploughed fields and the brilliant colours of the trees and berries. Even winter – the snowy woods, the sweeping wind, evenings spent indoors – had held its special pleasures. And then, of course, last term had been exciting because of the Dominick matinée and the fact that Drina had had the name part in the ballet called *The Changeling*.

Anyway, however much she minded, the time at Chalk Green was behind her and it was up to her to settle down quickly in London and work really hard, both at her dancing and at her school work.

"Drina!" called Mrs Chester, opening the door and switching on the light. "It's half-past seven. I know you don't want to be late on your first morning."

"I'm getting up now, Granny," Drina said, and heard her grandmother going into the kitchen to switch on the electric kettle.

Drina leaped out of bed and hurried to the bathroom to wash. She dressed hurriedly, and it was strange to put on a scarlet blouse instead of the emerald green worn at the residential school. Brushing her silky black hair, she stared at herself in the mirror. Her familiar self looked back at her, small, pale, dark-eyed. While most other people of her age were anxiously watching their height she had scarcely grown at all during the past year.

"Fourteen last November and I look *twelve!*" she said aloud, then drew the curtains and glanced out at the grey river and the roads and pavements white with frost. It was not fully light, but she could just see a string of barges passing under Lambeth Bridge.

As she joined her grandfather and grandmother at the breakfast table they both glanced at her anxiously.

"What's the matter?" Mrs Chester asked sharply. "Don't you feel well?"

"Quite well, thank you, Granny," Drina said firmly.

"She's just excited at the thought of going back to the Dominick," Mr Chester remarked.

"Scared would be nearer the truth," Drina confessed. "I'm afraid that things will be different. After all, I've been away for a long time."

"Well, eat a good breakfast. You can't go out on such a bitter morning with nothing in your stomach." Mrs Chester was a practical woman and had always felt it her duty to combat Drina's moods and fears.

"It's only the ballet class today and tomorrow," Drina pointed out. "School doesn't start properly until Thursday. I shall be home before eleven and this afternoon Rose is coming to tea. We may go for a walk."

"Yes, of course. She doesn't go to Chalk Green until tomorrow. A walk will do you good. But do eat that bacon."

Drina did her best but made a poor meal, and she was glad when she was waiting for her bus at the bottom of Whitehall. She got off at Kingsway and set off briskly towards Red Lion Square, swinging her little case, in which she carried her practice clothes, ballet shoes, a towel, and her most precious possession, a black cat mascot called Hansl.

She had just crossed High Holborn when she saw Daphne Daniety in front of her and she slackened her pace slightly. She and Daphne had known each other in their Willerbury days, when both had attended the Selswick Ballet School, but they had never been friends and things had grown worse lately because Daphne had been so jealous of Drina's part in *The Changeling*.

Unfortunately Daphne stopped to look in a shop window and a moment later she saw Drina. They gave each other doubtful smiles and could hardly walk on separately.

"So you're coming back?" Daphne asked. She was as fair as Drina was dark and much taller.

"Yes. I suppose I'll be in my old class. Who's going to take our ballet classes this term?"

"Miss Cranz, I think, and Miss Frame is going to be our form teacher again," Daphne told her, still rather stiffly.

"I don't know her well. Is she nice?"

"Oh, very. There's Queenie!" Daphne cried in relief as they reached Red Lion Square, and she ran ahead to join an arrogant-looking girl of fourteen who had given

Drina anything but a friendly look.

Drina followed them slowly, her heart rather heavy. She did not like Queenie Rothington, had never liked her since the day, two years before, when they had first met at the Dominick audition, but it always hurt her that they had to be enemies. The enmity was all on Queenie's side, but that did not make it any easier.

Queenie, even more than Daphne, resented Drina's most recent success and the fact that she had once had a dancing part in a West End play, for Queenie's mother – as she was never tired of pointing out – had been Beryl Bertram, once quite a well-known dancer, and Queenie put on airs and expected special treatment on that account.

"Oh, if only Rose were here!" Drina thought, pausing under the bare trees in the middle of the square to look across at the Dominick School and the building next door that was also the property of the Igor Dominick Company. There the Company had its rehearsal room.

"Not much of a place to look at, is it?" asked a voice at her side, and Drina, rather startled, swung round to see a very dark boy of about fifteen who was a complete stranger. But, since he wore the uniform of the Dominick School, he must belong.

Something about his tone made Drina say defensively, "I think it's very nice to look at, as a matter of fact."

He laughed and when he spoke again his voice was a trifle condescending. He spoke English well, but with a slight foreign accent.

"So I gathered. You were looking at it as though you owned it."

Drina was not normally touchy, but she felt unlike

herself that morning – cold, uneasy and apprehensive. It had been bad enough meeting Daphne and Queenie and now this unknown boy, with the handsome brown face and dark lashes far too thick and long for a boy, was being condescending, obviously thinking her very young.

"I *don't* own it and neither do you! But that doesn't stop me liking it. They always have both buildings painted in the Christmas holidays and I love the turquoise blue doors and windows."

He laughed again. "Don't be too sure that I don't own it! I might one day, anyhow."

Nonplussed, Drina decided to let it go. He seemed a most extraordinary boy and obviously yet another member of the School with a considerable opinion of himself. Basically humble herself, she never really knew how to deal with assured people, even if they were not much older than she was.

She ran across the road and up the steps into the entrance hall. The familiar smell of polish and winter warmth rushed at her and for a moment it was almost as though she had never spent two and a half terms at Chalk Green, with only one or two brief visits to Red Lion Square for rehearsals of *The Changeling*. There was her mother's portrait on the left-hand wall, with her ballet shoes in the glass case below. Elizabeth Ivory, one of the greatest ballet dancers ever known! And it was still a secret from nearly everyone, for Drina had vowed long ago that she would not try to build her own dancing career on the fact that she had had a famous mother.

Then suddenly a young woman she had never seen before came up to her, carrying a notebook.

"Name, please? You're new, aren't you?"

Drina stared at her, uncertain again. "No. At least, I've been at Chalk Green for nearly a year. I was here before that. I'm Drina Adams." She never used her full name, which was Andrina Adamo.

"Oh, of course! I did think I'd seen you somewhere. You were in *The Changeling* – had the name part. Then you know where to go. Your ballet class is in Studio Six."

In the cloakroom there were familiar faces. Betty and Jill rushed up to her, welcoming her back, and others from her old class seemed pleased to see her.

"Oh, Drina, aren't you glad to be back?" cried a girl called Lorna. "It must have been awful at Chalk Green! So cut off and lonely!"

"It was at first," Drina admitted. "But I got to like it." And, with startling suddenness, homesickness rushed over her and she thought of the Manor, all her friends there, and the way she had sometimes danced in the woods or on the smooth turf of the edge of the Chilterns. It was good to be back at the Dominick – of course it was, but she felt an outsider. There were so many unknown faces.

It was better once she stood at the *barre* and the familiar exercises began. She had never been taught by Miss Cranz before, but she looked a likeable person: small and dark with a vivid personality. Drina worked hard and earned a word of praise at the end of the class.

"You're the one who's been at Chalk Green, aren't you? Your *port de bras* are excellent."

"Dear little Drina! How delightful to have her back!" said Queenie under her breath and gave Drina an unfriendly look.

"We've missed her so much!" added Daphne, and Jill

said sharply:

"Oh, you two! It *is* nice to have her back."

On the way to the cloakroom after the class Drina met her old friend Jan Williams and his welcome warmed her heart.

"It's really nice to see you, Drina! No more exile at Chalk Green?"

"No," said Drina, a little sadly. "And, do you know, I know I'm going to miss it quite a lot! It seems so silly when I nearly broke my heart at leaving the Dominick."

"Oh, you'll settle in again in no time. I shouldn't worry."

In the cloakroom passage Lena Whiteway, the niece of a grown-up friend of Drina's, was talking to a group of older girls. She turned away from them to greet Drina.

"Oh, you're back, Drina! Aunt Adele told me you would be. How goes it?"

"I don't know," said Drina. "It feels odd."

"Ten months is a long time. But there's nowhere like the old Dominick."

No, there was nowhere like the Dominick, but, as Drina left the building in the midst of a chattering group, she still felt a little strange and out of things. If only Rose had been there! Betty and Jill were quite nice girls, though sometimes rather too friendly with Queenie and Daphne, and so were Lorna, Meryl and an Italian girl called Bello Giornio. But they were not Rose or Jenny.

She felt most unusually lonely as she set off down Kingsway and she found herself looking forward eagerly to Rose's arrival after lunch.

Rose arrived punctually at two-thirty and they took a bus to Hyde Park Corner. Striking out across the bare, wintry stretches of the park, Drina told her all about the morning at the Dominick and Rose listened with great attention, her pale face very sympathetic. She admired Drina a great deal, especially since she had learned her friend's secret. She would never be able to understand why Drina did not shout Elizabeth Ivory's name from the housetops. To have had such a famous mother and not to use the fact as a weapon to fight Queenie seemed to Rose little short of madness. But deep in her heart she had an inkling of the pride and independence that kept Drina silent.

"It must have been strange to go back, but you'll soon feel as though you've never been away. I envy you, really, though I do love Chalk Green now. Oh, Drina, I shall miss you tomorrow!"

"I missed *you* today. There were such a lot of strangers, and, oh, Rose! the oddest boy!" And she described the curious little conversation in Red Lion Square.

"Mother says that all boys who go in for ballet-dancing must be a bit peculiar," said Rose, laughing. "I often tell her she's wrong, of course. There's nothing in the least peculiar about Jan Williams or most of the others. What on earth did he mean about owning the School?"

"I don't know. I suppose he was teasing. He looked awfully – awfully arrogant. He was very good-looking, but I didn't like him much."

They walked so briskly, their pale faces gradually beginning to glow in the bitter air, that they soon reached the Round Pond in Kensington Gardens. The winter sun glowed back from the big sheet of wind-whipped water, and a number of ducks and other water-fowl were fighting for the bread that a small child was throwing.

Drina and Rose stood near by, laughing, and suddenly Drina was conscious that she felt much happier. She could hear the traffic in the distance and the Cockney voices of a group of playing children were shrill and familiar.

London! She thought of the great city spreading all about her and she remembered that she and her grandmother were going to the Dominick Theatre on Saturday afternoon.

"What's the matter?" asked Rose, noticing the change in her friend's expression.

"Nothing much. I suddenly got London back. I don't think I really wish I was still at Chalk Green, even if the Dominick is going to be difficult and a bit lonely at first."

Rose slipped her hand through her friend's arm. "I'm glad. I don't want you to be miserable."

"Oh, Rose, I wonder what will happen this year?"

"Anything might – to *you*. Perhaps you'll be in another play. And you said you might go to Italy to meet your Italian grandmother."

Drina sighed as they set off again towards the Broad Walk. "I can't imagine another play. I think it will mostly be hard work. Rose, I hope I don't go to Italy. At first I thought it would be exciting, but now I'm hopelessly scared whenever I think about it."

"But why? It would be wonderful to see Italy. You love travelling."

"I loved being in the Alps and I do like seeing new places. It's very satisfying and thrilling. But I don't think I want to stay with my Italian grandmother. I don't know anything about her. It seems so odd that my father was Italian."

"It must be odd," agreed Rose whose parents were both Londoners. "But it's very romantic."

"Perhaps Granny will change her mind. I don't think she's really a bit keen. When my father and mother died Signora Adamo wanted to take me and they had a quarrel about it. Grandfather told me that they write to each other now and that my Italian grandmother wants me to go and stay, but probably I never shall. I suppose I'm an awful coward, but it would mean going alone –"

"I only wish *I* could travel!" Rose said wistfully.

"Perhaps you will one day – with the Company," Drina remarked, and then they walked on in silence for some time, both thinking about the future.

2

A Letter from Italy

At dusk they returned to the flat for tea and soon afterwards Rose had to leave.

"Mother said I must be home early, because of going back to school tomorrow. I still have some packing to do, actually."

They looked at each other a trifle sadly, because it would mean not meeting again for some weeks.

"I'll come to the station with you, if Granny will let me," Drina said.

Mrs Chester never cared for Drina being out at night in winter but she gave her permission.

"Only don't be long. It's freezing hard, I think. I don't want you to get cold."

They went down in the lift and crossed the entrance hall of the large block of flats. Outside the pavements were certainly frost-covered and the lights seemed extra brilliant.

They crossed the road towards the dark gardens and walked slowly past the Houses of Parliament.

"I know Granny said hurry, but I do hate saying goodbye," Drina remarked. "I shall write at least once a week, really long letters. And you must tell me all the Chalk Green news, especially how Petrouchka is. Oh, and about Emilia's little sister, Bianca. You're having her with you in Ivory, remember."

"So long as we don't have Christine!" said Rose, referring to a girl whose temperament was very like that of Queenie Rothington.

"You won't. I don't believe Matron would do it. Emilia wants Bianca, and she'll be shy and strange, just arriving from Italy."

"And you'll tell me all the Dominick news?"

"Oh, I will. All the gossip. We may meet at a Dominick matinée quite soon. They're sure to bring you up before very long."

"If the weather isn't too bad."

"Remember the snow before Christmas!" Drina cried, as the chimes of Big Ben rang out immediately above them.

"I certainly do, and you lost in the woods with Petrouchka when you should have been in the bus on the way to London!"

Drina went with Rose into the warm atmosphere of the station and waited while she got a ticket to Earl's Court. Then they faced each other again, almost shy now that the moment of parting had definitely come.

"Good luck!" said Drina.

"And to you." Then Rose said violently, "I think partings are beastly!" and plunged down the steps without a backward glance.

Drina returned soberly to the open air. Partings certainly were depressing. It was the same when Jenny went home; worse, really, for she had known Jenny longer and could say things to her that she never could to Rose, fond of each other though they were.

Jenny had never cared for dancing and had given it up years before; all her interests centred on the country and farming. But that didn't seem to matter, nor, really, did their long absences from each other. Jenny was always the same – fair, rather plump and very sensible. She pretended to laugh at what she called the "half-lit world of ballet", but she knew all about Drina's hopes and fears.

Drina tramped back past the Houses of Parliament and Victoria Tower Gardens. Crossing the road, she thought suddenly of the Chiltern woods all about Chalk Green Manor and wondered where Petrouchka was at that moment. Probably in the gardener's cottage warming his stomach in front of a log fire, as he loved to do.

Ignoring the lift, she walked up the flights of stairs and she just had her key in the lock of the front door when her grandmother pulled it open.

"Here you are, Drina! I thought you'd got run over. Jenny's on the telephone."

"Oh, good!" And Drina flew to the telephone and spoke eagerly, glad that her grandmother had gone into the living-room and shut the door.

"Jenny! I was just thinking about you!"

Jenny's cheerful voice rang in her ears. "So was I. Wondering how you got on today. Mother said I might speak to you, though she's always moaning about the telephone bill. What's the matter?"

"How did you know anything was?" Drina demanded.

"My child, I can sense it. Gipsy Jenny, you know!"

"You'd have been burnt as a witch in the seventeenth century. Oh, it's nothing, really. I've just said goodbye to Rose, who's going back to Bucks tomorrow. And the Dominick was odd today. I felt almost an outsider."

"I *thought* you'd miss the country!"

"I do, but it isn't only that. I hate feeling like a new girl – at the Dominick, of all places!"

"Yes, it must be hateful, but it won't last. Your heart's at the Dominick doing *développés à la seconde en l'air* and *echappés sur les demi-pointes* and all the rest of it." Jenny's tone was so comic, and her accent so deliberately un-French, that Drina giggled.

"I don't know how you always make it sound silly."

"It *is* silly to the layman – or laywoman, or whatever it should be."

"And it's muddled. My heart can't do them!"

Far away in Warwickshire Jenny, too, giggled. "Well, you know what I mean. Anyway, don't be miserable. By the way, I had a good journey back and a simply whacking lunch. I adore lunch on the train, though Mother says that I could easily buy sandwiches at Paddington. Meals are so expensive now."

"When are you going to the farm?"

"I've been. Today. I went on the bus and walked two miles. They've got twin lambs and heaps of others expected. You'll have to come at Easter if that Italian business doesn't come off."

"I'd like to."

"I must go, or Mother will be mad. Cheer up!"

"I have already. You always make me feel better."

But the line had gone dead. Jenny, afraid of her mother's wrath, had hung up.

In the living-room Mr Chester was reading *The Times* and Mrs Chester was mending a pair of Drina's tights. She immediately handed them over to her granddaughter.

"You can do these, Drina. I don't know how you get such holes in the toes. You've no homework tonight?"

"No." Drina took the ballet tights obediently, though she loathed darning.

"What's the matter? You don't seem quite yourself today."

"Nothing, Granny. I'm fine." It was one thing Jenny being a "gipsy" and quite another when her grandmother started to be perspicacious.

"I thought you'd be in seventh heaven to find yourself back at the Dominick. What a strange child you are." Mrs Chester sounded faintly irritated. She had brought Drina up since she was little more than eighteen months old and almost counted her as her own child, but she found many occasions when she did not understand her.

"It was just a little odd. It'll be different tomorrow."

"Were there many new students?"

"I don't really know. There were a lot of strange faces, but I don't suppose all were new. There was a foreign boy I think was new –"

"What nationality?"

"I don't know. He spoke English very well, but with an accent. And he *looked* foreign. And there was a little dark girl in our class who was definitely new. I didn't notice her much at the time, but I remember her now. She was *very* foreign. I don't think she spoke much English. She looked rather unhappy."

"Talking about foreign countries," said Mrs Chester carefully, "I had a letter from Signora Adamo this morning."

Drina jumped and pricked her finger. Her grandmother tut-tutted at the sight of the spot of blood.

"Give it to me, Drina. You don't want blood all over it. I wish you weren't so nervy."

"I'm not. You surprised me. What did she say?"

"You may read it," said her grandmother, reaching for her expensive grey handbag and taking out an envelope with an Italian stamp.

Drina studied the postmark.

"*Milano. Republica Italiana.*" She found herself reluctant to read the letter, for it was true that she definitely shrank from the proposed visit. But after a moment she took the single sheet out of the envelope and spread it out.

Dear Mrs Chester wrote Signora Adamo, in a clear hand.

I was indeed very pleased to receive your letter and very happy to know that you and your husband were able to be back in England for Christmas. I was happy also to be informed that you are quite willing for Drina to visit here, later in the year. I am anxious to see and get to know my granddaughter, as you so well understand. It is strange to think of my son's child being now fourteen.

My daughter Giulia is, as perhaps I told you, married and now lives in Genoa. She has a daughter Antonia who is somewhat older than Drina. Antonia has expressed a great wish to meet her cousin.

I would wish to have Drina with me for perhaps one or two weeks and then perhaps she may go on to Genoa to stay with the Gardinos? My other son, of course, at present lives in Perugia, and he also has children. But no doubt Drina will make other visits once she has been to Italy.

You will arrange this first visit as soon as you find it possible, I know. Perhaps at Easter or else in the summer. The child cannot travel alone, but I have many acquaintances who travel often to London and no doubt an escort can be arranged. I note that you would prefer it if she did not fly.

I trust that your husband is now fully recovered from the unfortunate illness that sent him on the trip to Australia?

My best wishes to you both.

                    Yours very sincerely,
                         Andrina Adamo.

"How odd that we've got the same name!" Drina breathed. "And fancy having Italian cousins!" But dismay was the main emotion that filled her after having read the rather stiltedly phrased letter. She pictured her Italian grandmother as very "proper", with piled white hair and an awe-inspiring manner.

"Yes, fancy!" said Mrs Chester, without much enthusiasm. She had made up her mind that Drina must get to know the Italian relations, but could not enjoy the thought of the coming visit.

"*Need* I go, though? I'd sooner go to the farm at Easter. Jenny's awfully keen about it."

Mr Chester put down his paper and eyed her quizzically. "Do you mean to say you prefer mud and what Jenny calls muck to Italian sunshine and perhaps the blue Mediterranean?"

Drina's face had flushed. "I don't mind mud and all the rest of it now. I really do love the country. And I love the farm and my dear cat, Esmeralda. I could go to Italy in the summer, perhaps, or else next year."

"Well, we'll see," said Mrs Chester briskly. "You'd better get it over, I think. I should have thought you'd be thrilled. And your Italian grandmother certainly ought to see you."

It was never any use trying to argue with her grandmother, so Drina was silent. Once Mrs Chester had made up her mind to the visit there was probably no avoiding it. But two weeks alone in Milan with Signora Adamo was an alarming prospect and so was the thought of travelling with complete strangers.

Drina was glad when it was bedtime and she could go to her own room. She stood in her pink pyjamas, staring unseeingly at her little reproduction of one of Degas's ballet pictures. Her mind was teeming with rather troublesome thoughts. Almost a new girl at the Dominick . . . the unfriendliness of Queenie and Daphne . . . Rose off to Chalk Green alone . . . the rather alarming Italian grandmother.

"I *am* a coward!" she told herself gloomily. "I'm not shy in the ordinary way. I don't mind in the least dancing or acting in front of people. But I think I'm always a bit scared of new experiences. I like to know where I am . . . to be safe."

To her surprise she found, when she climbed into bed, that she was shedding a few desolate tears. Perhaps it was because, for a short time at least, the always magic and beloved Dominick School had lost some of its enchantment; because life seemed a trifle difficult and unsafe, making fresh demands on her.

She dried her eyes impatiently and took up her book. She was allowed to read for half an hour and always took full advantage of the privilege.

In the living-room Mrs Chester was putting into words some of Drina's own thoughts and feelings.

"She *is* an odd child! I never feel I fully understand her. I should have thought she'd have loved being back at the Dominick and as for the prospect of going to Italy for two or three weeks –"

"She's nervous about the unknown grandmother," her husband said quietly.

"Well, but she *is* a close relation, after all. I suppose it's partly my fault for that early quarrel. Otherwise she would have kept in touch with Drina and perhaps met her long ago. But Drina loves travelling. She adored the Swiss Alps and she wrote such vivid letters about the Welsh mountains last summer, when she was there with the Pilgrims –"

"She *knows* the Pilgrims. They're her second family. After all, it takes a lot of confidence to face strange people in an unknown country, without any support at all."

"But she *has* confidence. Think of her on the Dominick stage before Christmas, bowing and smiling and holding that bouquet. She might have been Betsy at the height of her fame."

"Dancing is different, I fancy, and she has had so many changes since she was twelve. Leaving Willerbury, having that one term at the Pakington School, going to the Dominick, then being moved to Chalk Green –"

"Now back to the Dominick? Oh, well, I'll say no more. Perhaps you're right. And she does seem to have developed a lot mentally, though she stays so small and slight. It's a troublesome age for girls."

"And Drina has the temperament of an artist."

"Yes. I wish she hadn't," said the woman who had never fully understood her own daughter, the red-haired Betsy who had become so great and famous as Elizabeth Ivory. "Or I wish Betsy had lived to cope with her."

"And have missed many happy years with the child?"

"We'd have had them both, but Betsy would have been responsible."

"It wasn't to be," he said, picking up *The Times* once more. "And Drina is a lovely girl."

"You spoil her," said his wife, but her voice was softer. Soon afterwards she rose and went to look in at her granddaughter.

"Time your light was out, Drina. Good night."

"Good night, Granny."

"And don't worry about the Dominick or Italy."

"I'll try not to." And Drina curled up under the Degas picture, feeling happier and more settled than she had done all day.

3

Strangers at the Dominick

The next morning was very frosty indeed and there was such a bitter wind that Drina shivered as she waited for the bus. Seagulls were screaming over the river and the sky was heavy and grey. But she felt more cheerful than on the previous morning and, instead of meeting Daphne as she walked up Kingsway, she met Meryl and Bella who greeted her warmly.

"How fast you walk, Drina! It seems funny when you're so small."

"Granny says I just skate along," Drina remarked. "She often asks if I'm with her or not! But it's too cold to go slowly, anyway."

"It's icy! And Meryl has got chilblains."

"On my heels," said Meryl gloomily. "They got worse after yesterday's class. It's agony! I don't know how I shall manage to dance."

"Miss Cranz will ask you if you sleep with a hot water bottle," said Bella, who spoke perfect English after three years in London. "She loathes hot water bottles. My sister, who had her last year, told me."

"I don't, anyway. It's just bad luck or a bad circulation or something. Horrible painful things!"

Drina, who had never had a chilblain in her life, had sympathetically dropped to a much slower pace to accompany the sufferer.

"It must be awful. But it seems odd when you get so much exercise."

"I'm not the only one. Marlene in the next class was moaning yesterday. But she *does* have hot water bottles. Two in this cold weather, she says."

They approached the Dominick chattering hard and Drina already felt a little less strange. How ridiculous that she had felt like a new girl!

In the hall they ran almost full tilt into Miss Janetta Selswick, who once owned the Selswick School in Willerbury and who now advised and sometimes taught at the Dominick. She smiled very warmly at Drina.

"So you're here again, my dear? It's nice to see you."

"It's nice to see *you*!" said Drina, who had once been in awe of Miss Selswick.

"Oh, I enjoy my London life. Have you seen Jenny Pilgrim lately?"

"Yes. She was staying with me until a day or two ago and she rang up last night. She'd been to her uncle's farm."

Miss Selswick laughed. "She'll have to become a farmer! She would certainly never have made a ballet dancer."

"She didn't want to, as you know. It was her mother."

"These mothers who want ballerina daughters!" said Miss Selswick, and laughed again as she passed on along the hall.

Meryl and Bella had gone on and Drina made her way slowly towards the flight of stairs that led down to the cloakrooms, boys to the left and girls to the right. There seemed to be unusual noise and she paused halfway down to stare in astonishment.

In the wide space at the foot of the stairs was a considerable crowd of students, most of them still in their outdoor clothes. In their midst were Jan Williams and two or three other boys of about the same age. They were facing a taller youth whom Drina recognised as the handsome boy who had spoken to her in the square the previous day. He had changed into practice clothes and was standing with his feet apart, his handsome head thrown back. He looked scornful, but somehow at bay.

"But it is true, I tell you. I greatly prefer the French. I had no wish to come to London. A great, dirty, sprawling city, while Paris –"

"We know what Paris is like," said Jan easily. "Some of us have been several times and a few of us *live* there. But now you're here, at the Dominick, and throwing your weight about remarkably vigorously for a newcomer. There's no need to criticise the cloakrooms and London and all of us."

"England, so I have always been told, is a free country, and one can therefore express an opinion. I would have preferred to remain in Paris, but my father thought otherwise and so I am here. And no doubt it is reasonable. Besides, I may criticise what is likely to be my own –"

"That's what he said!" a younger boy cried shrilly.

The dark boy's eyes were lit with sharp amusement. "After class yesterday I told several my name –"

"He said he was called Igor Dominick," a girl cried. "My brother told me."

"There's only one Igor Dominick," Meryl said,

swinging her case, "and he *is* the Dominick School!"

"And I am his only son. Do I have to keep on saying so?"

There was silence. Everyone stared and the boy from Paris stared back, shifting his dark gaze round the half-circle of curious, puzzled or disbelieving faces.

"I didn't know he had a son," said Jan, at last.

"Why should you know?" the young Igor Dominick asked, with that touch of arrogance that had got Drina's back up even in two minutes' conversation.

"But –"

"I surely don't have to produce my birth certificate?"

"Well, even if you are," said Jan cheerfully, "there's no need to put on airs. It doesn't make you any better or worse, I suppose. Time we all changed. The bell will be going."

Everyone began to disperse and Drina descended the last few stairs. She was as startled as everyone else. For it was true that no one had known that Igor Dominick, the man who controlled the Dominick School and Company, had a son. It seemed very strange and unexpected and at the back of her mind she was suddenly sorry for the boy from Paris. He had shrugged in a very foreign way and brushed past her, making no attempt to speak.

Perhaps it was true that he hated leaving Paris and was not in the least resigned to belonging to the Dominick, but it was silly of him to irritate everyone. He seemed to have a most unfortunate manner and the touch of arrogant amusement didn't help.

In one of the girls' cloakrooms Drina found everyone discussing the matter.

"Amazingly handsome, but *what* an opinion he's got of himself! Do you really think he's – ?"

"Must be, if he says so. Did you ever see a boy with such eyes? But if he's going to turn up his nose at the Dominick, and the next minute rub it in that he's going to be in charge one day –"

"– he'd better have stayed in Paris."

"Perhaps he'll go back there."

"He said his father had other ideas. Anyway, we shan't see much of him, since the boys have separate classes."

"Not school classes, though."

"Oh, well, he's older than most of *us*. Fifteen, at least."

They were still discussing the surprising new boy when they reached the studio. But then conversation had to stop as they started to warm up at the *barre*. Drina soon forgot all about him as she settled down to work, her eyes on Jill's straight back immediately in front. But halfway through the class, at the beginning of the centre practice, she noticed again the very small dark girl she had vaguely noted on the previous morning. The girl was accomplishing various *enchaînements* without much difficulty, but when Miss Cranz spoke to her she looked shy and worried.

"Plis, I speak ze English not bad sometimes. But zen it goes away."

Miss Cranz immediately dropped into French and was answered with more assurance. The class went on and Drina was for the most part too absorbed to think of the stranger again. Afterwards she stayed behind at Miss Cranz's request to answer a few questions about her time at Chalk Green, and by the time she approached the cloakroom stairs most people were on their way home.

Betty and Jill flew past her.

"We can't wait, Drina. We're going to Oxford Street to buy something for Jill's aunt."

Drina didn't mind. She had enjoyed the class and felt in no hurry to leave the building. Chalk Green already seemed far away, though it was so easy to imagine what was happening that morning. Nearly half past ten. Then Matron would be waiting for everyone to arrive and Rose and quite a number of the others would be on the train, halfway to Princes Risborough.

The cloakrooms were already almost deserted and Drina began in a leisurely way to change into her scarlet blouse, grey skirt and outdoor shoes. She was just ready to leave when she heard an unusual sound – it seemed like a muffled sob. The cloakrooms were divided by wooden partitions that did not quite reach the top and the sound seemed to come from a little distance away.

Drina picked up her case and gloves and hesitated. A few older girls departed, chattering, from the cloakroom nearest the stairs and the whole place suddenly seemed very quiet. In the silence she heard the sobbing again, muffled but definite.

She went along the narrow passage, peering into the next cloakroom, but it was quite empty, except for some outdoor clothes on the far peg. The last was a small one, rarely used, and in there, crouching close to the radiator, was a small figure, with curly black hair falling over a downbent face.

"Don't cry!" Drina said rather awkwardly, putting her hand on one thin shoulder. The child – but she was probably nearly as old as Drina herself, since she was in the same class – looked up in a startled way, but didn't stop crying. If anything her sobs increased.

"We'll probably get locked in or something," Drina

said. "*Do* come and finish dressing." She wondered if she ought to try and speak French, but the stranger gulped and then said:

"I come."

She followed Drina into the next cloakroom and began to change her shoes and put on her coat and scarf.

"I am zor-sorry. It is that I am so miser-able. Not to know – not to speak – And London so-so strange."

"You dance very well, though." There had been no doubt of the newcomer's command of her own body, her familiarity with the ballet movements.

"I love to dance. I shall like to be here. But all is so strange and I think of my father."

She was extremely pretty, in spite of her swollen eyes and unhappy expression. She had a little, almost heart-shaped face, with eyes far darker than Drina's own, and her features were all most attractive . . . the little nose, the firm chin and the wide, full mouth. Drina felt great pity for her and longed to help, but so far she was rather at sea.

"I don't understand, you know. Where is your father? What country do you come from?"

"I am Lynzonian." She shut her case and looked for her gloves. "My name is Ilonka Lorencz. My father is in Lynzonia and will come not."

"Oh!" Drina was by no means ignorant of the tragedies of Europe. There were three girls and a boy at Chalk Green who had, in their different ways, escaped from behind the Iron Curtain. In the little country of Lynzonia there had recently been a tragic and unsuccessful revolution against Soviet rule. "But you're not in England all alone? *Do* pick up your case and come. We really might get locked in."

The girl obeyed and they hurried up the stairs into the entrance hall where, as it happened, Marianne Volonaise herself was standing. Drina had not seen her since her return to the Dominick and she blushed to be caught in the building so late. But Miss Volonaise did not seem to mind.

"Well, Drina Adams? So you're back?"

"Yes, Madam." Miss Volonaise was generally "Madam" to the School.

"And glad to be here, I suppose?"

Drina smiled rather sheepishly, remembering the long conversation they had once had in the beechwood when she had still hated Chalk Green.

"Actually I miss Chalk Green. I-I *did* learn to love it."

"Oh, well, you can go back and see them all. And you really belong to us here."

Drina glowed. For Madam to say that, when she was still only an unimportant junior . . .

Marianne Volonaise's observant glance went to the red eyes and slightly puffy face of Drina's companion.

"And you've made friends with Ilonka? I'm sure Drina will look after you, Ilonka dear. She knows what it's like to be a stranger and homesick."

"Oh, I will!" Drina promised.

"Good! She'll need a friend. How long have you been in England, child?"

"But two weeks . . . three. Two days after Christmas I come." Ilonka bobbed an odd little curtsy.

"Oh, dear! Where were you at Christmas?"

"In Vien-na. It was so sad. But I was flew-flown –"

"Well, we're glad to have you. You show great promise." Then, as Ilonka looked puzzled, she said, smiling, "You dance well. It's in the family."

"Oh, zank you!"

Marianne Volonaise patted her shoulder and smiled warmly at Drina.

"Off you go. And I'm due in the rehearsal room." She watched them hurrying down the steps, standing with her elegant coat slung over her shoulders in the way she often wore it.

Out in the square Drina stopped. "Which way do you go? I'll walk a little way with you, if you like."

"We 'ave a flat with furniture near Bloomsbury Square."

"Oh, that's not far. I'll come with you."

"Zank you ver' much." Ilonka already looked a little more cheerful. "Do you live near?"

"I live in Westminster. That's by the Houses of Parliament and Big Ben."

"And ze Ab-bey. Yes, I know."

As they walked rather slowly along Ilonka poured out to Drina the stark and terrible story of her escape from Lynzonia. Her English was better than Drina had supposed at first and she explained that her mother had once lived in England, dancing with an English ballet company. Later she had returned to Lynzonia and married, and Ilonka had a sister of nearly seventeen, now in the Dominick Company. She had been in the Company for almost six months and was the youngest member.

"My mother wish to leave Lynzonia and return to Britain, and Terza she was to go also. It was so terrible – so wicked in our country, and we want to be free. My father say he will follow wiz me. Zey 'ave the terrible time, so often nearly caught, but in the end zey reach Vien-na and come to England. Terza she gets to be wiz ze Dominick Company. Zey say she dance so well and need not be in ze School. My mother she gets good work selling dresses in a big shop."

"And you and your father – ?" Drina prompted, trying to read between the lines of the story.

"My father not come, after all. But he send me wiz one of his friends. It was bad – I cried to leave him – but not so bad as for Terza. She was so long in hiding before she crossed the frontier and people were dead – dying, some shot. She was separated from Mother. Now – but that my father is not wiz us – we are very well. I have ze scholarship at the Dominick." Then she added slowly, "But Lon-don is so strange."

"Oh, dear! It must be." Drina felt such pity that she hardly knew what to say.

"I live here. Up in zis high building: only a little flat. Someone was so kind. You will come wiz me?"

Drina glanced at her watch. "I can't today. I live with my grandparents and Granny worries rather. I said I'd be home early. I will another day."

Ilonka's face was suddenly smiling. "You are nice, Drina. But not ver' English. You look –"

"My father was Italian. He's dead." And then Drina said goodbye and almost ran back to Kingsway to catch her bus.

Her mind was racing. It seemed to have been a long morning, and an eventful one, too. The boy from Paris, who said that his name was Igor Dominick . . . Ilonka Lorencz and her escape from Lynzonia . . .

There would certainly be plenty to tell Rose in her first letter.

"I shall write this afternoon," Drina thought, as she crossed Parliament Square.

4

A Matinée with Ilonka

Mrs Chester looked with some relief at Drina's much brighter face.

"Well, that's better! I thought you might be sickening for something yesterday."

"What a terrible thought, Granny!" Drina said, with a shudder. "I just can't do that. I've got to work hard this term."

"You always do work hard, so far as I can gather. Why especially this term?"

"Oh, being back at the Dominick and Miss Cranz seems to expect an awful lot."

At lunch, which she and her grandmother had alone, Drina told her about the strangers at the Dominick.

"There's a very handsome boy who says he's Igor Dominick's son. He seems to be getting everyone's back up, but I was a bit sorry for him. He's been living in Paris and going to a Ballet School there and evidently he didn't want to come to London, even though his father is here."

Mrs Chester frowned thoughtfully. "Hadn't you heard of him? I thought you knew everything about the ballet world."

"I thought I knew a lot," Drina said frankly. "But I

didn't even know that Mr Dominick was married."

"I believe I did know that, but I fancy his wife has been dead for many years. The boy may have been living with relatives, as I have the feeling that Mrs Dominick was French. Why is the poor lad upsetting people?"

"It's hard to say quite why. He's got an odd sort of manner. Very arrogant and critical. I don't suppose I shall see much of him, anyhow, as he's older. Then there's Ilonka." And she launched into a description of Ilonka's tears in the cloakroom and what she had learned of the Lynzonian girl's history.

"There are so many of these tragic cases," said Mrs Chester. "It must be very difficult for the mother. Why didn't the father come, after all? Was he stopped?"

"I don't know. Ilonka was crying about her father. I think I know which member of the *corps de ballet* her sister must be. I noticed last term that there was a new one who looked very young. Extremely dark and pretty and a good dancer."

"Lynzonians are sometimes quite fair, I believe," Mrs Chester remarked.

"Well, Ilonka isn't. She's darker than me. Her eyes are like those purply-black pansies."

"Really, Drina! How you exaggerate!"

"It's true. But perhaps you'll see her soon. May I ask her to tea?"

"Of course, if you want to. You know I like to meet your friends."

"She isn't a friend yet," Drina said soberly. "But I think she might be. Miss Volonaise asked me to look after her." Then at last Drina noticed that her grandmother did not look quite as usual. "What's the matter, Granny? Have you got a headache?"

"No, but I think it may be a slight chill," said Mrs Chester. "I shall go to bed this afternoon. I suppose you can find something to do?"

"Oh, of course. I'm sorry you don't feel well. I want to write a long letter to Rose, and then I may go and see Miss Whiteway."

"Don't stay out after dark. It's going to be foggy."

So Drina washed up and then settled down to write the letter to Rose, telling her of the happenings of that quite eventful morning and adding messages to Emilia, Hildegarde and the twins, whose dormitory she had shared in Ivory.

The next morning Mrs Chester was still unwell, but she insisted on getting up to cook the breakfast.

"It's nothing very much, but I'll stay indoors today. It's really too foggy to go out. Drina, be careful crossing the roads."

Drina set off cheerfully for her first school day at the Dominick, not in the least deterred by the fog. She rather liked the secret feeling that fog gave even to the most familiar and busy streets, and people slipped by strangely, as though they were on some unusual mission and not just going prosaically to work.

The fog was not so thick away from the river, and in Red Lion Square she could see many students making their way towards the Dominick building.

The boy from Paris was idling along alone and Drina, walking briskly, soon drew level. She looked at him doubtfully and then said, "Hullo!" and smiled.

Igor Dominick said "Hullo!" in return, but didn't show the slightest sign of wanting her company, so she hurried on, feeling a trifle humiliated. He almost certainly thought her one of the younger ones, and that was one disadvantage of being so small and slight. At fourteen Drina was beginning to wish at times that she looked older.

Marianne Volonaise was just coming down the stairs and, as Drina was hurrying along the entrance hall, she found herself beckoned.

"Drina, my dear, just a moment. I was glad to see you with Ilonka Lorencz yesterday. Perhaps she hasn't told you, but she and her family have had a very sad time."

"She told me that they escaped from Lynzonia, Miss Volonaise, but that her father was still there."

"Yes. Apparently he meant to get out, but the Communists grew suspicious and so he sent Ilonka with a neighbour. Poor child, I'm afraid it will take her a little time to settle in London. If you can help – someone of her own age may be more comfort than an adult, perhaps."

"I'll do what I can. I'm going to ask her to tea."

"Oh, good! We're all very anxious that she'll learn to be happier."

As she went on to the cloakrooms Drina thought, still with a faint sense of surprise though she had had many other indications, that it was nice of the great ones like Mr Dominick and Miss Volonaise to bother with the unimportant juniors. Once she had thought them utterly remote: distant beings who held everyone's fate in their hands, but who could not possibly recognise or care about each boy and girl in the Junior School.

But once she had changed into practice clothes for the ballet class that began each school day she had little time for contemplation. Ilonka was there and seemed very ready to attach herself to Drina, and they went along to the studio together, with Betty, Jill and Meryl close behind.

After the ballet class came an hour of writing out timetables and settling into their new desks. It seemed very strange to Drina to be sitting in the large classroom overlooking the square, when for so long she had worked in the old and beautiful rooms of Chalk Green Manor, with the beechwoods encroaching to within a hundred yards of the house.

During break she and Ilonka drank milk in a corner and Ilonka told her a little about Terza.

"She so much likes to dance with the Dominick Company. Terza is hap-py to be in London. She is to be in ze new ballet."

"What new ballet?" Drina asked.

"Ze new one zey rehearse soon. Three acts it has and ver' English."

"Oh!" Miss Adele Whiteway had said something about an important new ballet for which she was designing the sets and costumes, but unfortunately Drina had had to leave because of the fog just when the conversation was getting interesting.

"It's for the European tour," Jill remarked, attaching herself to them. She was curious about Ilonka, especially since she had realised that the pretty youngest member of the Company was Ilonka's sister. "One of the seniors was saying something about it yesterday. They're going to France and Spain and some other countries in April and this is to be something very special. Very English, as Ilonka says. They're starting rehearsals next month."

"What's it called?" Drina asked, but Jill didn't know and Ilonka thought it was something about a Princess.

"I shall have to go and see Miss Whiteway again and

hear all about it," Drina remarked.

She went home for lunch, as she generally did, though many of the pupils stayed to have soup and sandwiches in the canteen, and, returning, she saw some members of the Company going into the rehearsal room next door. Peter Bernoise, the principal male dancer, was just parking his car and Bettina Moore, a young dancer who had always attracted Drina, was standing on the pavement, talking to other members of the *corps de ballet*. They were all muffled up in thick coats and scarves and by no means looked like the glamorous beings who floated across the Dominick stage. But for Drina they had an endless fascination and she ran up the steps of the School feeling pleased and oddly stimulated.

After all, it was thrilling to be back in Red Lion Square; thrilling to be nearer the centre of things, to remember that in that ordinary-looking building next door, ballets were being born that perhaps would be shown in many countries.

If only she might know for certain that one day she herself might be a member of the Company! But there was no way of knowing, and all that any of them could do was to work hard and hope that the longed-for thing might happen.

Because of the fog Drina was not able to go home with Ilonka, but they left the Dominick together and walked as far as the top of Kingsway. Ilonka didn't like the fog and buried her small pale face in her scarlet scarf, but she seemed a trifle happier than she had done the day before, even after a bewildering time in the classroom.

"Everyone is so kind. Miss Frame she tell – told me not to worry."

"No, don't worry," Drina said warmly. "I'm sure it will be all right, Ilonka." And she hoped most fervently, as she hurried homewards, that all would in the end be well with her attractive new friend.

Mrs Chester said on Friday morning: "I'm afraid I shan't be well enough to go to the Dominick Theatre with you tomorrow afternoon, Drina. I think you'd better ask someone to go with you."

"Oh, Granny, I'm sorry. But I don't suppose *you* are very."

Her grandmother smiled wryly. "No, not very. It's not a programme that appeals to me, and, as you know, I always watch ballet slightly under sufferance."

"I do wish you didn't, but I suppose one can't change people," Drina said sadly.

"No, I don't want to change at my time of life," Mrs Chester retorted, though she was by no means as old as the remark seemed to suggest. "Why don't you ask Ilonka to go with you?"

"I might. She hasn't seen the Dominick yet, even though her sister is dancing with them. May I bring her home to tea afterwards? Will you be well enough for that?"

"Oh, yes. It's just that I don't want to go out in the cold just yet."

So Ilonka was invited to use the ticket and also to go to tea at the flat and she seemed very pleased. They arranged to meet outside the theatre on the next afternoon and Drina set off from the flat in very high spirits, though fog still lingered by the river and the air was raw. She adored going to the theatre and especially loved the Igor Dominick Theatre. Even the Royal Opera House, with its impressive atmosphere, its huge stage and sweeping red curtain had not quite the magic of the Dominick Theatre for Drina. At the Dominick her own mother had danced on many, many occasions, had danced there on that last fatal night before the flight to America on which she had lost her life. And only just before Christmas Drina had danced there in the ballet called *The Changeling*.

Walking briskly along the Victoria Embankment Drina remembered that wonderful afternoon with a faint shiver of excitement and happiness. It had been marvellous! Just for a very short time she had almost imagined herself a ballerina! Of course the real thing was still unimaginably far away – she might never achieve ballerina status at all – but nothing could take away the satisfying memory of pushing her way through the folds of blue curtain, standing there curtsying to the audience.

"I wonder *when* I shall dance on a stage again?" she mused as she approached the Igor Dominick Theatre. "Perhaps not until the matinée next December. Perhaps not then, because I mightn't be chosen."

Ilonka was not waiting, so she stood for a few moments looking at the poster that advertised that afternoon's programme: *Façade*, *Le Spectre de la Rose*, *Peter and the Wolf* and one of Igor Dominick's short ballets.

Ilonka arrived with a rush, the ends of her scarf flying, and they went into the theatre. When Drina and Rose went to a matinée alone, either at the Dominick or Covent Garden, they usually went in the cheap seats, for Rose, at least, was not well off and she had to save hard to be able to afford theatres at all. But this afternoon the seats were in the centre of the front row of the circle and they took their places happily.

Apart from dancing, Drina rarely felt so happy as when she sat in a theatre during those minutes before the overture started, and she never wished to talk. But Ilonka was looking round eagerly and asking to have things explained. After all, it was the first time she had ever been in an English theatre and Drina did her best to imagine what it must feel like.

Ilonka had seen *Le Spectre de la Rose*, but the other ballets were all strange to her, though of course she knew Prokofiev's music for *Peter and the Wolf*, and after a time they bent their dark heads over their programmes.

"Fancy! Bettina Moore is the Duck!" Drina cried. "She's had very few solo *rôles* so far, because she's still quite young. Only eighteen or nineteen. She used to be a lovely Little Clara in *Casse Noisette*."

"Zat I should like to be," said Ilonka.

"Oh, so should I. I dreamed I was Little Clara the other night. I wonder what our first solo *rôles* will be?"

Ilonka shrugged and sighed. "It's not easy to – to im-ag-ine."

"No, it isn't. Sometimes I'm afraid I may never have a real solo *rôle* at all. Perhaps I shall live and die in the *corps de ballet*."

"But no."

"But yes. Why not?"

Ilonka looked at her new friend earnestly. "Because you have ze look of a true dancer."

It was not the first time that the same compliment had been paid to Drina, but she flushed with pleasure.

"Oh, I do hope you're right, Ilonka!"

Then the house lights went down and the spoken introduction to *Peter and the Wolf* began, the Voice telling the audience that each character in the ballet would be represented by one of the instruments in the orchestra. And Ilonka sat forward on the edge of her seat, giving a faint chuckle as each instrument responded to the Voice.

It was odd to be with someone who was almost a stranger, instead of with Rose, but Drina was pleased to see that Ilonka was happy. And she settled down to enjoy the lively Prokofiev music and the humour of the ballet. Peter was a lively figure, but Drina watched the Duck with especial interest. Lucky, lucky Bettina down there on that big stage! She was still far from dancing major *rôles* in the great classical ballets, but she was well started on her career.

"I wish I could get to know her!" Drina thought as the ballet ended with the Duck, restored to life after being "swallowed" by the Wolf, joining the others.

"It was so fun-ny!" Ilonka cried, clapping hard. "But me I like best those ballets zat are beautiful and sad."

"I do, too, really," Drina agreed. "I think I love *The Sleeping Beauty* best, though it's not really sad, just so perfect in places that I always want to cry. I shall always love *Les Sylphides* especially. It's the very first ballet I ever saw, and that was on television when I was small."

All the same they enjoyed the short dances in *Façade*.

"It's very attractive!" said Drina. "Particularly the Yodelling Song."

Le Spectre de la Rose was, however, more to their taste and Drina always drifted away on the romantic music to that secret world in which she was almost down on the stage with the dancers. It happened to her sometimes and was an experience that she treasured and consciously waited for. While it lasted it was very easy to imagine herself great and famous, holding a vast audience with her perfect movements. But it was only a dream experience and she recognised that clearly, being a realist at heart where her future was concerned and therefore all the more frightened of the uncertainties and difficulties.

The programme ended with the short Igor Dominick ballet, in which most of the Company, wearing black and silver, danced to very modern music. Catherine Colby, the ballerina, wore silver tights and a close fitting black bodice, and she danced with such abandonment that both girls sat forward stiffly, scarcely even blinking.

Amongst the dancers was Ilonka's sister Terza, and, as they all acknowledged the wild applause at the end of the ballet, Drina used her opera glasses to take a good look at her.

"I can tell she's like you, even with make-up on and wearing that tight silver cap. She has your shaped face and the same eyes. Oh, Ilonka! That was exciting, wasn't it? Even though I don't really like very modern ballets with jangly music so well as the older ones."

"It was ver' good," said Ilonka.

They left the theatre and set off through the misty dusk towards Westminster, and Drina felt warm and happy, as she always did after watching ballet.

London in the winter . . . the smell of the river . . . towers and spires in the fading light. Suddenly she tucked her hand into Ilonka's arm.

"You *will* learn to like London, Ilonka. There's nowhere quite like it. Sometimes I love it so much that I don't know what to do!"

"But it is ver' big and ver' strange," said Ilonka.

5

The new Ballet

Ilonka continued to find London "ver' big and ver' strange", and there were times when she seemed very unhappy, but there were things that she enjoyed, too. After a week or two she confessed to Drina that she liked being at the Dominick, where the atmosphere was much freer than at her dancing school in Lynzonia. Many people at the Dominick knew something of her story and nearly everyone was kind and friendly. Even Queenie and Daphne, neither renowned for warm humanity, were quite pleasant, though they rarely spoke to Ilonka when she was with Drina.

"They don't like me," Drina told her. "It makes life very difficult."

"Zey are jeal-ous. Zey are so cross because you dance well and have ze good parts. Queenie's muzzer – mother was, she tells me, a ballerina, but zat is no reason –"

"Oh, we never hear the end of Beryl Bertram," Drina sighed and then hoped that Ilonka would not think her catty. But Ilonka seemed to understand. She was very quick and sensitive.

"My mother also was a ballerina before Terza and I were born. But it makes *me* no better and it does not make Queenie."

"That's what I think," Drina agreed, but she sighed.
again, for there were times when it was a sore
temptation to tell the world that Elizabeth Ivory was
her mother. It was now over two years since she had
learned the surprising fact – one evening at Covent
Garden, when she and her grandmother had been
talking to a ballet critic, Mr Colin Amberdown – but she
had never yet yielded to that sometimes almost
overmastering longing.

"And I never shall," she thought. "Not until I have
some idea of what is going to happen to me, anyway. I
will *not* have people saying, 'She's Ivory's daughter, so
she must be good!' Or, worse still, 'She's Ivory's
daughter, so wouldn't you think she'd show more
promise?' I couldn't bear either. But oh! I should love
to see Queenie's face if I told her!"

Drina's friendship with Ilonka was well on the way
to being established. Mrs Chester had taken a liking to
the Lynzonian girl, remarking that she had very good
manners and had obviously been well brought up. Mrs
Chester was a snob at heart and she did not relish –
though she knew better than to interfere – the fact that
Drina met all sorts at the Dominick School and did not
seem to mind. Mrs Chester was fond of Rose, but
never ceased slightly to regret that her parents were
poor and that she came from a small and overcrowded
house.

Drina, in her turn, had visited the flat near
Bloomsbury Square and had come very close to loving
Mrs Lorencz at their first meeting. Ilonka's mother was
beautiful, in a slightly tragic way, with huge dark eyes
and soft black hair. She had a lovely figure and wore
her clothes so well that it was small wonder she had

managed to get a good job in a fashionable store. She still had something of the look of a dancer and Drina listened with interest to her stories of her life as a dancer, in London, Paris and, for a time, in her own country.

Terza, too, was very attractive and it was difficult sometimes to remember the months of fear and deprivation she had gone through.

Mrs Lorencz and Terza never spoke of those times to Drina, but Ilonka did sometimes and Drina gradually learned more about their life in Lynzonia, their yearning to escape to a freer country and the plans that had been made. Ilonka spoke of her father only with difficulty, and small wonder, for it seemed that they might never see him again. News had been received through some other Lynzonian refugees that he had been put in prison after Ilonka was got safely over the frontier.

"He wishes not to be a Communist, my father," Ilonka said sadly. "Oh, Drina, perhaps I should have stayed with him. But then –"

"He wouldn't have wanted you to stay. He'll like to think of you safe in London. If he knows," Drina added to herself, for it was possible that Mr Lorencz had never learned that his younger daughter had reached Vienna and later arrived safely in London.

After the first week or so Drina felt perfectly at home at the Dominick again, though she still often thought of Chalk Green and tried to picture the snowy woods, her friends struggling up through the drifts to the hill's edge above the Vale of Aylesbury, and the little brick-and-flint cottages of the village with the blue wood-smoke drifting over them.

Rose wrote regularly and her letters were packed with gossip.

I often think of you at the Dominick, she wrote, early in February, when most of England was shivering under a prolonged cold spell. *Ilonka sounds nice and I'm glad you've made friends with her. It must be terrible for her not knowing if she'll ever see her father again. And I'm dying to see Igor Dominick Junior. Perhaps I shall when we get up for a matinée, but it won't be yet, for we're almost snowed up. The younger ones had a terrific snow-battle yesterday. It was quite exciting.*

Emilia's sister Bianca is really an awfully nice kid, though her English isn't very good yet. She fits in very well in Ivory. Hildegarde twisted her ankle in the woods a day or two ago and can't dance, so she is in an awful state about it. Matron said rather crossly that one would think she had lost a leg and would never be able to dance again!

Yesterday we took Petrouchka with us to the farm and he just adores the snow. He seems more used to it now than he was before Christmas.

Everywhere looks lovely. The larches are almost red in some lights and the grey trunks of the beeches are always beautiful, I think. Do you remember when I first arrived at Chalk Green and how frightened I was of the country?

All the same, though I love it now, I often wish I was with you, able to go to the theatre whenever I've saved up enough, and seeing the Company leaving the rehearsal room. I wish I'd seen Bettina Moore as the Duck in Peter. But perhaps I shall before the season ends, and they set off on their tour. I hope so, anyway, and I hope we meet soon.
> *Lots of love from*
> *Rose.*

And Drina wrote back:

Dear Rose,

Thank you for your long letter. It's pretty snowy here, too, and Granny gets bothered that I'll catch cold, but I haven't so far, though lots of them have colds and flu. There were ten away in our class yesterday and Miss Frame says she loathes this term. Queenie was one of them. She has a bad throat and Daphne looks quite lost without her.

Ilonka, Betty, Jill and I had a snow-fight with some of the boys after the heavy fall yesterday and one snowball went wide and landed flat in Peter Bernoise's face. He was just coming out of the rehearsal room. He was really nice about it, but we felt very small. Two minutes later Catherine Colby came out and slipped on a hard bit of snow. She did the most graceful slide and ended up with a bump. As she got up she said, 'Thank heavens there aren't any news cameras about! I can just see the headlines — "Ballerina takes a toss in Red Lion Square".' I picked up her case and she said, 'Thank you, Drina!' which staggered me, as I don't know how she could possibly have got to know my name. I didn't know the Company knew we existed.

Then Jan and the other boys saw Igor Dominick Junior coming back from his lunch and snowballed him, but he just held his head higher than usual and stalked past. He is an odd boy, and he doesn't seem to get any more friendly. He always seems to be alone and I should think he's miserable, but he's never let on. They say he's a wonderful dancer, though. I can't help feeling a bit curious about him, but I don't suppose I shall ever get to know him better.

The Company have started rehearsing the new ballet. It's called The Lonely Princess and is full length. The *music is arrangements of English folk tunes and Miss Whiteway played some of them to me and then the variations on them. It is about a sixteen-year-old Princess. In the first scene she is in the schoolroom, with her six prim governesses, then suddenly she realises that she is almost grown up and says she won't do lessons any more and wants some friends. The King and Queen decide that it is time she was betrothed then, but she scorns all the important Princes – rather like Belle Rose in* The Prince of the Pagodas. *She runs away to have some fun and to get to know ordinary people.*

Act Two, Scene One, is in the woods, where the village young men and girls are gathering flowers for their May Day Festival, and she meets a young man in green whom she thinks is a woodcutter. But she doesn't care a bit and falls in love with him. They both go on to the village green and the Princess is crowned May Queen because the girl who should have been is ill. She has four attendants, who have a lovely dance, Miss Whiteway says, to a beautiful tune called Lull Me Beyond Thee. *There are all the things they used to have at English village festivals, only turned into ballet. A maypole dance, and morris men, and a Jack in the Green and a hobby-horse. And then the May Queen dances with the woodcutter and everyone crowds round and congratulates them. But the King and Queen turn up and of course the Princess has to go back to the Palace. But of course it all ends happily, because the woodcutter is really a Prince, and the last act is the wedding, when the Princess asks all the village folk, and her four May Queen attendants are bridesmaids.*

Most ballet stories sound silly when you tell them, as you know, but Miss Whiteway's settings are lovely. I've seen the models – very simple and bright. The choreography is by that young man called James Crofter, who has done several short ballets for the Dominick. Miss W. says the village scene is best, and that he has been very clever in interpreting a morris dance and the maypole dance in ballet movements.

What a long letter! I must stop and do my homework. It's snowing again, Granny says.

Love from
Drina.

The new ballet was certainly a source of interest to the School, for it was the first full-length ballet created by the Company for a long time. The press, too, was interested and there were several news items about it, including a rather scathing comment from a well-known ballet critic that anything so English could hardly appeal to continental audiences.

Ilonka's sister was to be in it, as a lady-in-waiting to the Princess and Catherine Colby was to dance the Princess.

"I wonder if we'll get a chance to see it before they take it abroad?" Drina mused. It was very thrilling to be so near the place where a ballet was being born, and when, one day towards the end of February, Miss Lane, the headmistress, asked her to take a note in to Miss Volonaise, Drina was astonished at her luck.

She had only rarely been into the rehearsal room, though on one never-to-be-forgotten occasion she and Rose had climbed on a roof to look through a window and been caught by Igor Dominick himself.

It was pleasant to slip her red-lined cloak about her and to go up the steps of the building next door, but she felt rather shy as she walked down the passage. A beautiful tune came to her ears, a tune that seemed old and strange, and when she pushed open the door she saw what seemed to be the whole Company. They were not all dancing, though; some were merely sitting about with extra sweaters knotted round their shoulders. About twenty were dancing; a section of the *corps de ballet*, as Drina saw at a glance. It was difficult to tell when they all wore practice costume just what part of the ballet it was, but she made a shrewd guess at the village youths and maidens.

Her glance travelled slowly round the huge room, as she stood there in the doorway, with her cloak hanging from her shoulders. Igor Dominick himself was there, standing by the piano in a characteristic attitude. He was a handsome man, with thick greying hair, a high forehead and very blue eyes. Patently the young Igor Dominick took more after his mother than after his father, and yet there was a distinct resemblance, more of stance and the carriage of the head than anything else.

Of Miss Volonaise there was at first no sign; then Drina sighted her in a far corner, talking to Peter Bernoise and Catherine Colby. She approached very shyly indeed, for the first time almost wishing that she had not met the headmistress in the corridor and been entrusted with the note. Miss Volonaise had her back to her, but Catherine Colby gave Drina a quick look and murmured a few words.

"A note from Miss Lane, Madam," Drina said, and was turning away when Catherine Colby asked:

"This is your Changeling, isn't it? I wish I'd seen that ballet."

Drina flushed deeply, but her heart lifted with astonished rapture. It had been amazing to know that Catherine Colby knew her name, but to find her interested in *The Changeling*!

Marianne Volonaise smiled, with her hand on Drina's shoulder. "Yes. I believe you saw her in *Argument in Paris*?" That was the play Drina once had a part in for a few wonderful weeks.

"Yes, I did. She was very good. Are you going to do some more acting?"

"Oh, no," Drina said. "That was just – just an accident. I want to dance."

"Of course she wants to dance!" Miss Volonaise said cheerfully. "We don't want to lose her to the straight theatre. How do you like this dance, Drina? From the new ballet. The village lads and girls –"

"In the woods," said Drina, greatly daring, and Madam laughed.

"Yes, in the woods. I see you know something about it."

"Miss Whiteway told me the story and played some of the music to me."

"Yes, of course. She's a friend of yours, isn't she?"

"She showed me the models of the sets, too, and the designs for the costumes. I love them."

"You'll have to see the ballet."

"I want to, of course, but I thought it was for the tour."

"Oh, we'll give it in London for a short time, beforehand. You can see it then."

Drina went back to the Dominick School with a singing heart. It was so wonderful to be noticed, even so briefly. She was filled with a delight that was all the greater because she was so intrinsically humble.

"They're nice!" she thought. "I'm sure Catherine Colby's nice. She's so pretty and kind and natural, even though she's famous."

She was still faintly lit with the pleasure of those

moments in the Dominick rehearsal room when she returned to the flat for tea, but her happiness soon received a severe jolt. Her grandmother remarked:

"I had another letter from Signora Adamo today, Drina, and she agrees with me that it will be best for you to go to Milan at Easter. You have more than three weeks' holiday and Easter is very late. It will be an ideal time to visit Italy and will set you up after this bad weather. You're looking very peaky."

Drina stared at her in dismay. "Oh, Granny, must I? I don't think I want to go at all. I want to go to the farm with Jenny. She said in her last letter how much she was looking forward to it."

"You can visit the farm in the summer," Mrs Chester said. "I think we must definitely get this Italian visit fixed for as soon as possible. Otherwise Signora Adamo will think I'm being obstructive. She's very anxious to see you."

Drina said no more, but felt utterly dismayed. It would be wonderful to see Milan . . . Genoa . . . the Mediterranean. Wonderful to be in Italian sunshine and to see such places as Milan Cathedral and the splendid palaces in Genoa, of which Emilia, who was a native of the city, had told her. There were the little places along the Riviera coast, too: Nervi, Camogli, San Fruttuoso. Emilia had talked of them and Camogli sounded lovely, with its picturesque harbour, its bright boats and "skyscraper" houses.

But oh! Not with a terrifying grandmother she had never seen and knew almost nothing about! Not even with an unknown aunt and cousin!

"Don't be ridiculous, Drina! Why are you looking like that? I should have expected you to leap at the chance."

Drina faced her squarely.

"I'm scared. I'm horribly shy about it. I don't think I've got the courage. They may not speak much English, and I-I don't know such a frightful lot of Italian. Emilia taught me some —"

"I telephoned Miss Lane today and asked if she could arrange for you to have some Italian conversation. She said it would be simple to arrange, as some of the senior students take Italian. I thought you liked new experiences?"

"Some I do," Drina said sadly. "But I'm afraid I shall just dread and dread going to stay with – with my other grandmother. We may not even *like* each other and I don't know the first thing about my father. Except that he was a businessman, with an office in London."

Mrs Chester said rather grimly, "I can tell you rather more than that. I suppose I should have done before, but I never saw much of him. He died, as you know, when you were only nine months old. Now, Drina, I shall expect you to be sensible and co-operative about this. Fourteen is old enough to enjoy meeting new people. You're not a child any more."

"No, Granny." But Drina went off to her own room feeling very dismal indeed. In many ways she still felt very childish and there was no doubt that it would be an ordeal to stay with the unknown grandmother in a foreign city.

"At least April is still a long way away," she thought.

6

Diary of a Dancer

Mr Chester was distressed to realise that Drina was not looking forward to the Italian visit.

"Couldn't it be put off until the summer?" he asked his wife. "After all, she has had such a lot of changes and she does look forward to seeing Jenny."

Mrs Chester sighed rather impatiently.

"You know I'm not in the least keen about it. I'm possessive enough to want to keep Drina to myself. She's almost certain to enjoy herself, once she gets over the first strangeness, and then we'll have her wanting to run off to Italy every holiday. But the business has gone so far that we can't draw back now, and I don't believe it would be good for Drina if we did. She ought to be encouraged to develop, and I'm really most surprised that she's shrinking from this trip to Milan and perhaps to Genoa."

"Well, I'm not," said Mr Chester, who had occasionally wished, throughout a long and mainly happy married life, that his wife was gifted with more imagination. "It will be rather an ordeal, and it must be strange for Drina to remember that she's half-Italian. She's so thoroughly English —"

"As to that, I doubt it. There are many things in her

temperament that seem to me more Italian than British. She has never been quite as sensible and balanced as I would like, and she has moods that I never have understood."

"So did Betsy," he said very quietly, "and she was wholly English."

Mrs Chester was silent for a few moments, then she smiled wryly.

"Yes, that's true. But she never had a temper like Drina's."

"We haven't seen it lately."

"No, but it's there. She can be very passionate. Betsy never lost control. If Drina *is* going to become a dancer – and she can conceive of no other life, more's the pity – then the kindest thing we can do is to make her independent and capable of coping with frequent changes. My natural feeling is to want to protect her, especially as she still looks a trifle delicate at times, but I see it wouldn't be wise. No, she shall go to Italy in April. It will benefit her health and widen her horizon. After all, going to Chalk Green worked wonders. She has more interests now and isn't always buried in ballet books. Last night I noticed she was reading rather a stiff-looking book about folk customs and last week it was one on architecture. She reads a lot of plays, too. She was quite excited over that secondhand volume of Barrie she bought recently."

"I fancy we can thank Miss Volonaise for that. You remember what Drina told us in one of her letters last year? She really is trying to think of other things besides the world of ballet. Oh, well, if you're set on it, my dear, we'll say no more."

"I think it had better be definite. I must start seeing about some new clothes for her. The spring things are in the shops and Drina pays for good dressing. It won't be very warm in Northern Italy at Easter, but she must have some pretty clothes. Italians can be extremely smart."

Drina herself was doing her best to forget all about the Italian visit. She had written to Jenny to say that the chances of their meeting before the summer were slender, unless Jenny could manage a brief weekend. And Jenny wrote back sadly, but obviously much envied Drina her chance of seeing another country.

Mother says I can come up one Friday night until Sunday, if that is all right with your grandmother? We just must have one meeting between now and summer. Letters and the telephone aren't the same, are they?

No, they were not the same and Drina longed to see Jenny. Sometimes she wanted her company so much that she wished the proposed weekend might be soon.

She had started the Italian conversation lessons and really quite enjoyed them, for Emilia had given her a taste for the language and Drina was very quick. But, apart from that, she really did try to forget that the end of term would bring an important new experience.

She was very happy at the Dominick, enjoying both ordinary lessons and ballet classes, and she was holding her own with the other pupils of the same age. But there was no doubt that the spring term was rather a trying one and she often felt more tired than she would have confessed. As February turned to March the weather was appalling and, though florists' windows were wonderful with spring flowers, spring itself seemed far away.

Drina stayed to lunch at the Dominick during the

wettest, coldest days and quite enjoyed it, as it gave her a chance to see more of the other members of the school. In the canteen she could watch the young Igor Dominick, though she never spoke to him, and listen to the conversation of the senior students, some of whom would soon be transferred to the Company or would find work with other ballet companies.

London, at least, was well provided with ballet entertainment during those dismal weeks and scarcely a Saturday passed without Drina going to the theatre, sometimes with the rest of the School and sometimes with Ilonka or her grandmother. On one occasion she saw a Russian Dance Company and took great pleasure in their gaiety and spontaneity, the brilliant colours of the costumes and the slightly alien music. But Mrs Chester, who accompanied her, was not enthusiastic.

"It was quite charming, but I always think that these folk dances and festivals transferred to the theatre become rather too much of a good thing. There have been so many companies from other countries, and folk dancing is basically a thing to be done, not watched –"

"Of, of course I'd sooner have classical ballet," Drina agreed. "But I love the colour and the music."

With Ilonka she went to see a Jewish Ballet Company and was deeply moved and impressed by its strangeness and sincerity, once she had got over the surprise of finding that half the *corps de ballet* were men with beards, bare feet and what looked rather too like nightgowns.

"I loved the announcer," she told her grandmother afterwards. "He had a beautiful voice and he made it all seem so important and meaningful. But I shall be glad to see *Coppélia* and *Les Patineurs* next week with the school."

Coppélia was always one of her favourite ballets. She loved the Mazurka and Czardas in the first act and the "mechanical toys" in the second, and Catherine Colby was always a delightful, mischievous Swanilda.

"I'd love to dance Swanilda one day," Drina said to Ilonka, who loved the ballet, too. "But I don't think I should ever be really good. I have a feeling that, if I ever have the chance, I'll be better in more serious *rôles*. Oh, Ilonka, think of dancing Giselle!"

"So difficult," said Ilonka.

"Oh, I know. One of the most difficult *rôles*. There's such a great contrast between the first and second act."

Soon after that Ilonka was away from the Dominick with a bad cold and Drina missed her very much, for they had grown to be good friends. Ilonka was not always sad and serious by any means, though she had her very bad times when she was obviously thinking of her father, from whom there had been no news at all. She could be very amusing and had a lively sense of humour, and so had Terza. Drina enjoyed visiting the Lorenczs' flat and it seemed strange not to have Ilonka to walk home with, as she usually did when the weather was not too bad.

Ilonka was scarcely back when Drina herself caught a bad chill and she was confined indoors for over a week.

"I do so hate missing classes, Granny. I simply can't afford to!"

"You aren't the only one, by any means," said her grandmother quite cheerfully. "And as for school work, you can get on with it very well here."

"I know. But it's dismal alone."

But Drina did work quite hard when she felt rather better. She developed a troublesome cough and Mrs

Chester would not hear of a return to the Dominick.

"Wait two or three days. I don't want you down with pneumonia."

During this time Drina read the newspapers more carefully than usual and one day she was reading a Book Page when she gave a cry of astonishment.

"But it can't be – I didn't know! Look, Granny!"

Mrs Chester put on her spectacles and looked at the publisher's advertisement.

"*Diary of a Dancer* by Terza Lorencz, Blane & Marshton Ltd: 'The moving story of a young dancer's escape from behind the Iron Curtain.' Is it Ilonka's sister?"

"It must be. But I don't know anything about it. How very odd!"

Ilonka came to see Drina that afternoon after school and she nodded when questioned about the book.

"Yes, it is Terza's diary. She wrote it in Lynzonia and then later, when she was in hiding, waiting to cross the frontier. Afterwards in Vienna and then in London, when she was first accepted by the Dominick Company." Ilonka's English had improved and was now nearly fluent.

"But, Ilonka, why didn't you tell me? A real book!"

Ilonka was rather self-conscious.

"Terza is shy about it now that it is to be published. Mother, you see, knew Mr Blane long ago when she lived in England, and it was he who helped us to find the flat. He heard about the diary, and then he read it and said it should be read by other people."

"But – wasn't it written in Lynzonian?"

"In French, actually. Terza always loved to speak and write French. And Mr Blane himself translated it."

"And it's out on Saturday? I shall buy it, of course."

"No, Drina, I will ask Terza to give you a copy."

"Of course not. I still have one of my Christmas book tokens. I thought there might be something I wanted badly later on – I do badly want Terza's diary."

And while she listened to the Dominick gossip Drina was still marvelling to herself about the book.

"I never knew a real author before," she said as Ilonka was leaving.

"But it is just a diary, just as it was kept. Mr Blane only – only edited it a very little."

"I still think it's wonderful. No one will ever want to publish *my* diary. Not that I keep a proper one," added Drina. "I start every January and soon let it lapse."

On Saturday morning she was allowed to go out for the first time, since the sun was shining at last, and she went straight to her favourite bookshop in Victoria Street, the same one where she had first met Miss Adele Whiteway soon after her arrival in London. The window had an impressive display of *Diary of a Dancer*, with a cardboard ballet dancer bearing a slight resemblance to Terza Lorencz.

Drina's friend, the bookseller, remarked, as he wrapped up the book, "The publishers think it will be a bestseller. They think it will cause as much stir as *The Diary of Anne Frank*."

Drina called in to see Miss Whiteway and then went home to start the book. She was still reading at teatime, her black hair falling over her face and her shoulders hunched. More than once she had hastily wiped away a tear, for it would never do for her grandmother to see her crying over a book.

The diary had gripped her from almost the first page, gripped her with a depth of pity and pain that she had rarely experienced before. It was exciting, too, and

somewhat surprisingly, very funny in places. Even in the midst of desperate fear, catastrophe and death Terza had sometimes managed to see the funny side of the things that were happening to her and the people about her. Like the young German Jewish girl in the attic in Amsterdam, Terza had the gift of painting people and their ways with a sharp, clear choice of words, but unlike Anne Frank she had lived to find herself in a free country, able to carry on with the thing she cared most about in the world, apart from the fate of her country and those dearest to her – her dancing.

It was not only Terza. In the early pages especially there was much about her father and mother and Ilonka, and Drina could very clearly picture their home and the political atmosphere that had made them all feel they must escape.

The book was somehow a shattering emotional experience. It seemed unbelievable that she, Drina, had met Terza Lorencz quite often, had sat at the tea table with her and even joked with her. That the whole family had had many tragic experiences Drina had known, but the terse, vivid phrases brought the whole thing most startlingly to almost unbearable life.

She read the last page as Mrs Chester said a trifle sharply, "You'll grow round-shouldered if you sit like that, Drina. Isn't it time you stopped now?"

Drina sighed and shut the book, then opened it again to have another look at the many excellent pictures. There was one of Terza and Ilonka as small children, several of the whole family, and a frontispiece of Terza, obviously taken very recently. There was also a press photograph of Terza and other refugees leaving Vienna by plane, and several of her dancing with the Dominick Company.

"Granny, it's wonderful! Shall you read it?" She hoped fervently that if her grandmother did read the book she would not dismiss it casually. That would be unbearable.

"I dare say. I think one should try to understand the experiences that others have in this modern world. Leave it for me and I may start it tonight."

Drina did her best to come back to reality, but her thoughts were far away all through tea and for most of the rest of the evening.

The Sunday papers, especially *The Observer*, were loud in their praise of the book, and by the end of the week it was clearly well on the way to being a bestseller. Every bookshop window seemed to carry a display, there were photographs of Terza and her mother and sister in many papers, and offers were streaming in for the translation rights.

The book was a nine days' wonder at the Dominick and Ilonka was very nearly overcome. Terza herself vowed that she would stay indoors and not face the world at all, but she had to dance with the Company as usual and was besieged in her dressing-room.

"If it's really made into a play, will you be asked to act in it?" Drina asked.

Terza shook her dark head. Her hair was straight and smooth, not curly like Ilonka's.

"But no. I can't act at all, that I know. I'm a dancer, not an actress."

"But it ought to be *you*. It's yours. It belongs to you." Drina felt a fierce interest in the fate of the book and the suggested play. For a time she scarcely thought of the coming trip to Italy. It seemed to have shrunk in importance.

7

Dress Rehearsal

Jenny came to London for the last weekend in March. Drina went to Paddington to meet her on Friday evening, glad that at last she was going to see her dearest friend again. It seemed a very long time since that morning in January when she had waved Jenny away. A good deal seemed to have happened in the months between: schoolwork, dancing, new friends, new clothes.

"I always feel a slightly different me," Drina thought, a trifle sadly. "But Jenny is always the same, or seems to be." Still, though she was conscious of growing and changing, it never made the slightest difference to their relationship. They could probably be separated for a year or more and yet take up their friendship where it left off. As Jenny sometimes said, they were like sisters.

The train arrived and the passengers began to stream along the platform. Drina felt a slight sense of panic, because she couldn't see Jenny and might miss her, but then she spied the familiar rather plump figure in dark blue, clutching a small grey suitcase. Jenny had grown even in three months.

"Hullo, my duck! Small as ever! It *is* nice to see you!"

"It's lovely to see *you!*" Drina cried.

"And London smells just the same. Paddington, anyway. Are we going by Tube? I've only got a light case."

"No, taxi. Granny said that guests must be properly received, though I told her, as usual, that you like the Tube."

"Still, I like taxis, too, though they always seem a terrible extravagance. You can see more from them."

All the same, Jenny didn't seem to have much chance to take in the London scene – she was talking much too hard, telling Drina all the Willerbury gossip.

"I saw Joy Kelly yesterday. She still goes to the Selswick School, only it's called the Marten-Clare School now. She doesn't like it so well as when Miss Selswick had it. And Mark Playford twisted his knee in the playground at school, so he's off dancing. He says there's a chance he may try for the Dominick, as he's got an aunt in London and he's almost definitely decided to go in for dancing properly."

"I wish he'd come," Drina said eagerly. "I liked him so much."

"And I went to the farm last weekend. It was superb. One of those unexpectedly soft and warm spring days. I milked and did heaps of mucking-out."

Drina shouted with laughter and the taxi driver looked round and said something under his breath.

"Oh, Jenny, I never quite get used to you! Mucking-out seems such a strange pleasure."

"I thought you understood about the country now? After Chalk Green."

"I do – in a way. I love walking in the woods and wandering over the hills, and learning about flowers and trees, and seeing the way the seasons change. And

I don't mind the mud any more or farm smells. But I still shouldn't like to clean out cowsheds or stables, and as for pigs – ugh!"

"Pigs are really quite clean animals. It's ducks and geese I'm not keen on for that," Jenny said robustly. "They *are* messy."

"Oh, Jenny! I don't know anyone but you who'd clean out anything."

"That's why I'm so good for you," Jenny said cheerfully. "I keep you down to earth."

"I *am* down to earth. I've worked like anything all term."

"You look a bit paler than usual and such a scrap. Aren't you ever going to grow?"

"I've grown half an inch," Drina said with dignity. "As a matter of fact I'm rather tired of looking so childish. When you're nearly fourteen and a half it can be rather humiliating."

"Never mind. You'll be thrilled to look young when you're thirty."

"Thirty? Oh, Jenny, shall we ever be so old?"

"Nothing more certain. Unless we die young."

"Oh, I do hope we don't die. It would be so awful to miss things, even being thirty and almost old."

"We wouldn't know anything about it."

"But we might, unless we were in a plane that fell into the sea, like the one my mother was in," Drina said. "I like to think that she was asleep and never knew what was happening."

Jenny gave her a quick look. "Well, we won't talk about dying. How silly it is! We're both very much alive and you're off to Italy in a very short time. Not flying there, are you?"

"No," Drina said gloomily. "My Italian grandmother

has arranged for me to travel with two people she knows. Signor Carletti is coming here on business and bringing his wife and they're taking me back. It'll be Dover to Calais and then one of the through trains to Milan, I think. Granny says it'll probably be the Lötschberg Line, and I shall like seeing the Swiss Alps again, anyway. Through the tunnel near Kandersteg and then down into the Rhône Valley. Then the Simplon Tunnel and Lake Maggiore. Otherwise I'm dreading the whole thing."

The taxi was speeding down Whitehall and they would soon be at the flat.

"I can see that you must feel strange about your Italian grandmother," said Jenny sympathetically. "But you'll enjoy it once you settle down."

"I wish I could think so. I go all cold and peculiar whenever I think of Signora Adamo. I don't mind going to Genoa so much, because there'll be a cousin of nearly my own age. And I'm going to meet Emilia from Chalk Green. She lives there, you know."

Then they were outside the big block of flats and Drina paid the driver. They went up in the lift and Mrs Chester met them at the door of the flat. After that, for some considerable time, there was little chance of private conversation.

But that night they sat in their pyjamas and talked for an hour, and it was just as though they had never been separated at all.

Next day they crammed in all the things that Jenny liked best – a walk along the Embankment to Chelsea and beyond, lunch in a restaurant, a quick look at Madame Tussaud's and a new film, set on a farm in Kent. Jenny adored the farming film, which she pronounced more sensible than usual.

"They did cram in rather too many disasters – to make the story exciting, I suppose – but he was quite a sensible man. I hate the soppy ones, who neglect their farms for their girlfriends."

And Drina laughed at the characteristic remark. "I still think that when you fall in love with a farmer you'll want him to desert his farm occasionally and walk in the spring woods with you."

Jenny said soberly, as they pushed their way along the pavement in Leicester Square, "What if I fall in love with another sort of person? A businessman, for instance? It would be the most frightful tragedy!"

"Or a ballet dancer," Drina suggested.

"That I never shall. I don't meet any except you. Never any male ones."

"You meet Mark Playford."

"But he's only fourteen!" Jenny protested, rather scandalised.

"So are you. But he'll be twenty when you're twenty and twenty-five –"

But Jenny would not consider such an absurd idea. "I don't care. It will never be Mark, nice though he is."

That evening Ilonka came to the flat to meet Jenny and Drina was relieved that they seemed to get on quite well. Jenny knew all about *Diary of a Dancer* and had even read the book, since her mother had bought it. She had been more moved by it than she would have cared to admit.

"She's very pretty and funny," Jenny said to Drina, when they had seen Ilonka on to the bus. "It does seem odd that she's the one in the book. The little sister who said she would never leave her cat."

"Ilonka never mentions that cat," Drina said. "I

suppose she'll never know what happened to him."

Their time together on Sunday seemed very short, for Jenny had to go home by an afternoon train, to be ready for school the next morning.

"Now mind you enjoy Italy," she said as they made their way to Paddington – by Tube that time.

"I almost wish I'd catch something and not be able to go," Drina said quite fiercely.

"Oh, rubbish! The more you get to know foreign countries the better. You'll feel at home when you go on tour with the Dominick. By the way, when *do* they go on tour this year?"

"In two or three weeks' time, I think. They're going to Spain and France and Switzerland – Basle and Zurich, I think – *and* Italy."

"Not when you're there?"

"I don't think so. I haven't seen the programme. I'm sure France and Spain have always been mentioned first. But they *are* going to Milan."

"You'll go with them one day, so remember that."

As usual Drina felt rather desolate when she had waved Jenny's train away, but there were several things to look forward to. The best thing was really that the whole Dominick School was to watch the dress rehearsal of *The Lonely Princess*, and Drina also had a hope that she might go to Chalk Green. The residential school broke up two days after the Dominick and her grandfather had said that he might take a day off from work and drive her to Buckinghamshire. It would be lovely to see the Manor again, Petrouchka and all her friends, even though, only a couple of days later, she would be setting off on the dreaded Italian holiday.

On the Monday morning Drina came face to face with Marianne Volonaise in an upper corridor and the Director of the School smiled at her.

"Well, Drina? How are the Italian lessons going? Miss Lane told me that you were having them."

"Quite well, thank you, Madam. I think it's a lovely language."

"You're going to Italy these holidays?"

"Yes. For nearly three weeks."

"Lucky girl! But you don't sound very pleased about it."

"I'm not. I want to see Italy, but I'm going to stay with – with strange relations."

Marianne Volonaise looked at her with interest. She did not know that Drina's real name was Adamo, but it had always been obvious that the child had some foreign blood.

"Whereabouts? Southern Italy?"

"No, not the South, though my – the family come from near Rome originally. Milan, and then I'm going on to Genoa."

Miss Volonaise laughed.

"Well, cheer up, child! You won't be alone. It's rather an odd coincidence, but we'll be there, too. On the 16th."

Drina went perfectly white and then her cheeks flamed scarlet.

"But – but I thought it was Spain first?"

"It all had to be altered. It was a terrible muddle, but now it's sorted out. We're dancing in Milan for a week and then going on to Genoa."

"*Oh!* How perfectly wonderful. Then I'm glad I didn't get in a panic about it. I'm glad it wasn't left until the summer. I shan't feel nearly so lonely when you're all there." Then Drina suddenly felt shy and rather silly. What would Madam think of such extravagant rapture? But she had meant every word. The Dominick in Milan! In Genoa!

But Miss Volonaise did not seem surprised.

"You'll have to come and see us."

Drina almost danced on her way along the corridor – she felt so much happier than she had done five minutes before. Suddenly life was exciting and satisfying, not filled with vague uneasiness and fright. The Dominick in Italy! Then nothing else really mattered. It would be wonderful to see them at La Scala, and perhaps at the Opera House in Genoa.

Two mornings later she sat with all the other pupils from the school in the circle at the Igor Dominick Theatre, waiting for the curtain to rise on the dress rehearsal of *The Lonely Princess*. Lessons were forgotten and everyone was very excited, keyed up.

"It'll be so dreadful," said Jill, "if it isn't a success. It's cost simply thousands."

"Terza thinks it a good ballet," said Ilonka. "She loves the music, though it is strange to her. So very English."

The overture was certainly fascinating, made up as it was of many of the airs used throughout the ballet. Drina found herself as usual sinking down into a happy state of anticipation and, as the blue curtain swished upwards, she sat forward, clasping her hands.

It was odd to see the real set, after the tiny model that Miss Whiteway had shown her. The one for the first act was very plain, as befitted a schoolroom. The three great windows looked out at the deep woods, with just a glimpse of the village in the distance.

Catherine Colby, as Princess Lucinda, was sitting at a huge table with piles of books in front of her and the six governesses were all trying to force her to learn. She sighed and yawned and suddenly leaped up, pushed all the books on to the floor and did a wild little dance round the table. Then she darted to each window and looked out at the world she scarcely knew. Gradually her rebellion mounted and the six governesses were sent away by the King and Queen. So now, they mimed to their daughter, you are grown up and must shortly marry.

The next scene was in another room of the Palace and the Princes were introduced one by one to the Princess. The Italian Prince, the German Prince, the French Prince and the Russian Prince. They were all in turn rejected and they did a skilful *pas de quatre* before departing sadly. The Princess, longing for fun and friends of her own age, decided to run away, through the woods and out into the sun.

"I think the Princes' *pas de quatre* was marvellous!" cried Betty, with shining eyes.

"And the Princess's first solo. She looked so young and rebellious –"

"Yes, it was good. So were the governesses. I liked their *pas de six*."

The first scene of the second act was in the depth of the woods. At first the village lads and maidens were dancing joyously; then, when they disappeared, the "woodcutter" had a solo. Peter Bernoise was famous for his elevation and some of his leaps drew gasps from the younger members of the School. Then Lucinda appeared and danced alone, while the woodcutter hid behind a tree, and after that they had a long *pas de deux*.

There was some delay before the second scene, as apparently something had gone wrong with Jack in the Green. Drina and Ilonka, who had somehow captured seats in the front row of the circle, clearly heard Mr Dominick and the Company ballet mistress discussing the matter of Jack's green "cage". However, the curtain eventually rose on the village green, with the brilliant ribbons of the maypole being threaded into a close pattern by twelve of the lads and maidens, while the others danced gaily at the front of the stage.

To the right was a flower-decked throne, but soon it was apparent that there was no May Queen. Princess Lucinda and her escort arrived very opportunely and the village folk, enchanted by her beauty, at once indicated that she must be their Queen. Then followed the crowning ceremony, which was performed by the Prince disguised as a woodcutter, and the four maids of honour – the smallest and youngest members of the *corps de ballet*, except for Terza, who was one of the Princess's attendants at Court – performed a very simple but charming *pas de quatre* to music that filled Drina with quick delight. It was the tune that Miss Whiteway had once played to her. After that came the dance of the morris men, their bells ringing and their big white handkerchiefs waving, the traditional morris movements very cleverly interpreted in terms of ballet. The fool leaped all over the stage, mingling with the crowd and urging the morris men to leap higher, and then Jack in the Green and the hobby-horse danced to the uninhibited cries of joy of the ten-year-olds in the first class of the School.

The King and Queen interrupted the festivities, trying to urge their daughter to return to the Palace and very dismayed at her declaration of love for a poor woodcutter. However, all was well, for the woodcutter declared himself a Prince, and villagers, morris men, Jack and the hobby-horse danced round the royal party.

The third act, in the best traditions of ballet, was the wedding scene, with Court and village happily mingling and a clever *divertissement* to entertain the happy pair of lovers.

As the music died away and the blue curtain came swishing down, Drina found herself, as so often happened, only just able to struggle back to the real world. She had loved the new ballet, whatever the critics might say about it after its first performance two nights hence, and it was astonishing to think that the next time she saw it might be in Milan.

"Because I shall *have* to go," she said to Ilonka. "It will be dreadful if my – my relations don't care for ballet. But I *must* go, whatever happens!"

8

Drina Travels

The Dominick School broke up for the Easter holidays on a lovely day in early April. Bloomsbury Square was filled with crocuses, and when Drina crossed the Mall on her way through St. James's Park to Westminster the daffodils were full out.

She frequently varied her way home on fine days, for she was a good walker and London delighted her at all times. In the park there were flowering trees, the lake shone in the sun and people had a more leisurely air than they had had for a very long time.

It seemed a pity to go indoors and Drina lingered by the water, watching the water-fowl as she loved to do. The lively little London sparrows twittered and milled about her feet, though she had nothing to give them, and she stood there happily, savouring the first real warmth and colour of spring. For so long the wind had been cold, and idly watching London scenes an almost forgotten pleasure.

England in April! And she was going to Italy and missing it all.

"I always love April so!" she cried to herself. "And the farm is so lovely. I shall miss the cherry-blossom in Warwickshire and all the other blossom, too."

Milan, of course, was a great industrial city and her grandmother lived in a flat not very far from the Piazza del Duomo – that much Drina knew. She had found a book about Italy in the library and read about the Cathedral and about the church of Santa Maria delle Grazie. The famous painting of *The Last Supper* was in the Refectory near by. She had read of La Scala, too, of course, on many other occasions, since it was the home of some of the world's finest opera and ballet.

Opera was so far almost unknown to Drina, except for *Carmen* which she had once seen at Covent Garden with her grandmother, but she had read about it with the same interest that she extended to the straight theatre, concerts and almost all forms of entertainment.

Mr Chester was as good as his word and the next day he planned to drive his wife and Drina to Buckinghamshire. They would have lunch in High Wycombe or Princes Risborough and then Drina could spend a couple of hours with her friends at Chalk Green Manor.

It was another lovely day and Drina was very excited to think of seeing the Manor again and the spring woods. It was probably too early for the beech trees to be in leaf, but there would be primroses and violets everywhere. It seemed a very long time since she had been in the country.

They had lunch in High Wycombe and then drove on along the road that was so familiar to Drina. She constantly pointed out landmarks – West Wycombe Church and Mausoleum on the hill; the long ridge that held so many of the villages and hamlets that she loved, Looseley Row, Redlands End, Speen and Great Hampden; and the delightful village of Bradenham close to the main road, with its brick-and-flint cottages and warm russet roofs, and its manor house and church beyond the big green.

"Oh, isn't it beautiful?" she kept on crying, looking at the pale chalky fields that she had learned to love so much, the shrill spring green here and there, the soft grey of the beech-trunks and the new feathery growth on the larches. When they turned up towards Bledlow Ridge she could hardly sit still.

"That hill like an upturned boat is Lodge Hill. It's so heavenly in summer: Rose and I often lay up there. No one ever goes. There's wild candytuft and stonecrop on top and all round the bottom thyme and orchids and poppies and centuary – all the chalk flowers."

"What are these pale green things in the hedge?" Mr Chester asked, surprised by her country knowledge. There was a time when Drina knew few flowers.

"Parson in the Pulpit. Cuckoo Pint. Lords and Ladies. It has lots of names. Wild Arum, too, I think. In the autumn the berries turn bright scarlet – a lovely colour."

The tiny hamlet of Chalk Green was passed and they turned into the Manor drive. The board by the gate announced that the Manor was a residential ballet school and Drina remembered that terrible day more than a year before when she and her grandmother had arrived by taxi. She had been cold and shy and utterly miserable, and it was strange to think how comparatively soon she had learned to love Chalk Green.

Halfway up the drive they met Rose, Emilia, Hildegarde and a younger dark girl whom Drina easily recognised as Emilia's sister, Bianca – she was so like Emilia. Mr Chester stopped the car and the moment Drina jumped out, talking eagerly, Petrouchka rushed out of the bushes to give her a rapturous welcome. Drina caught him up in her arms and hugged him violently.

Then she introduced her friends to her grandparents and after a few moments Mr Chester said:

"We'll go for a drive, perhaps out to Thame and Aylesbury, and meet you by the gate at four o'clock."

Talking hard, they all turned towards the Manor and Drina constantly stopped to caress Petrouchka, who could not get over his astonished rapture at finding his mistress again. Though he had about ninety other devoted mistresses, he had always regarded Drina as his own property, for it was she who had found him injured on the hill by Bledlow Cross.

Drina insisted on going all over the Manor and lingered for some time in Ivory, the room where she had slept for two and a half terms. She met the twins again, Joan and Sue, and many other old friends, including Jan's little Welsh cousin, Bronwen Jones. She met Christine, too, in an upper corridor, but Christine merely gave her an unfriendly look. She was very like Queenie Rothington at the Dominick and had never forgiven Drina for being chosen to dance the name part in the ballet called *The Changeling*. Miss Sutherland, the head of Chalk Green, gave her a warm welcome, and so did several other members of the staff.

It was some time before Drina and Rose could escape, but about three o'clock they did so with Petrouchka, and they took the path that led high on to Wain Hill. As they climbed through the woods Drina stopped often to admire primroses and violets and delicate wood sorrel and wood anemones.

"Oh, Rose! I feel as though I've never been away! It's so heavenly to see you and everyone again. And this country is just as secret and kind of magic as I remember."

Drina had certainly not forgotten the little lost paths through the woods and presently it was she who pushed her way through the tangle of bushes to the exact spot on the hill's edge where they would be above the small chalk splash of Bledlow Cross. Out on the smooth turf high above the Vale she gave a cry of delight, shading her eyes to gaze far away over the fields and villages in the plain.

"I've thought of it so often. The last time I saw it was on that snowy afternoon before Christmas."

"It was snowy nearly all through January and February, too," said Rose.

They sat on the right arm of the Cross while Petrouchka slipped and slithered on its steep surface. Presently he went off into the tangle of wild privet, dogwood and spindle below and they could hear him snorting contentedly as he nosed about in search of rabbits or other likely prey.

"He just loves to hunt," said Rose with a slight shudder. She had more than once been the recipient of some small corpse.

Presently Drina stretched backwards on the short sweet tuft of the hill, with her arms behind her head and her face upturned to the sun.

"The first time you lie on the earth each year is perfect, don't you think?" she said dreamily. "It makes me forget all my troubles, though I'm still horribly scared about Italy. My stomach seems to turn over every time I remember it, even though the Dominick Company will be there."

"I do envy you, all the same. Crossing the Channel, and France, and arriving in Milan. I shall think of you often," said Rose whose own holiday would be spent at home in London.

"Think of me coping with my Italian grandmother, then. You don't know how odd it is to know that there's a whole other half of you. I suppose I *must* have an Italian half, if I've got so many relatives in Italy, but I don't know where it is."

"I do," Rose said.

"Well, where?"

"In your Italian temper, and your love of music and colour."

"But *you* love those things, too, though you haven't got a temper."

"I don't love them quite as you do. Not so – so passionately. You'll probably come back quite foreign."

"I shan't, then," Drina said decidedly and soon afterwards they stood up, stretched and, calling Petrouchka, scrambled down the exceedingly steep slope to the Icknield Way below.

"What time shall you get home tomorrow?" Drina asked as they hurried back to the Manor.

"In the morning. I'm with the party that leaves at ten."

"Then come and see me in the afternoon, do. It may help to keep my jitters at bay."

Mr and Mrs Chester were waiting in the car when Drina ran down the drive at ten past four and soon they were speeding back to London through the bright afternoon.

"There can't be anywhere so beautiful as England!" Drina cried, and then added, "Unless it's Switzerland."

"Or Wales," remarked her grandfather. "You'll be saying the same about Italy perhaps, this time next week."

"I may think Milan interesting and exciting," said Drina. "But I don't believe I shall think it beautiful."

"Genoa is beautiful in many ways – a city of great contrasts."

"Emilia says so, too. I want to see Genoa." And then Drina lapsed into silence.

She scarcely slept on her last night at home and she looked so pale at breakfast time that Mrs Chester was very disturbed, though she made very little comment.

The cases were packed with all that Drina might need in Italy and, as she was provided with plenty of travellers' cheques and *lire*, she would be able to buy anything else that she needed.

"I expect, though, that Signora Adamo will want to buy you one or two things," said Mrs Chester, who did not relish the idea but was determined to be generous towards the woman who had lost the long-ago battle over who should bring up the orphaned child. "Now let me look in your shoulder-bag. Have you got everything? Show me! Your passport, your tickets and reservations? The travellers' cheques and *lire*, and the French francs for meals on the train? Yes, all behind the zip, so they should be quite safe. Remember to put your passport back each time you've shown it."

"Yes, Granny," said Drina meekly, wishing that her stomach would behave more reliably. It felt empty and peculiar.

She told herself fiercely that many of the pupils at the Dominick flew all over Europe, and even as far as Australia and New Zealand. But *they* were going home and not to visit total strangers: it made a lot of difference.

By half past eleven she was wandering restlessly

about the flat, wearing her new dark red jacket and white blouse. Her cases stood in the hall, labelled: "Miss Drina Adamo, passenger to Milan, Italy. Via Dover, Calais and Lotschberg Line." Her grandfather had said that it was better to put Adamo, as that was the name on her passport. On top of the cases were her gloves that exactly matched her jacket, her grey coat, for Mrs Chester had insisted that it might be very cold on the boat and that Northern Italy was not always warm in spring, and the new leather shoulder-bag that was a present from her grandfather.

"I hope you're ready in time!" said Mrs Chester, with faint sarcasm. "We don't want to be at Victoria until at least ten past twelve. Twenty minutes to get settled on the train is plenty of time."

"I know. But I've nothing else to do," said Drina and was thankful when the telephone rang and it was Rose, to wish her a good journey.

They went to Victoria by taxi and Mrs Chester soon spied Signor Carletti and his wife by the barrier. He was a tall, distinguished-looking grey-haired man and his wife was very smartly dressed and with pretty silvery hair. They greeted Drina in such perfect English that she felt somewhat relieved, for she had been imagining having to try to speak Italian all the way to Milan, and they were very cordial to Mrs Chester.

Mrs Chester had no intention of lingering, however. She kissed Drina briskly and said, "I'll let you get on the train, then. Be a sensible girl, Drina, and write often."

"Yes, Granny." Drina suddenly felt passionately attached to the calm, grey-haired woman who was almost like her mother. It would have been easy to burst into tears or to beg not to have to go after all, but both would have been childish and undignified. She managed a rather stiff smile and followed the Carlettis through the barrier.

An hour or so later she was looking out at the April fields of Kent, where blossom foamed round the farms and tall oasthouses and the earth was, in places, as white and chalky as in the Chilterns.

The boat train rocked on its way towards Dover and presently the blue Channel appeared in the distance.

By that time Drina was enjoying the excitement of travel and she had decided that she liked the Carlettis very much. After all, it was thrilling to be on her way to a foreign country and in the morning – before the meeting with her grandmother at the Stazione Centrale, Milan – there would be a sight of the snow-clad Alps.

"I expect I've been a terrible baby and a coward," she thought. "I believe I shall enjoy *some* of it, anyway."

And she did enjoy almost every moment of her long journey: the calm, blue crossing . . . the arrival at Calais . . . meals on the train . . . settling down in her sleeper as dusk fell and lying there, hearing the great train roaring through the night. She felt suspended between two worlds, in a sort of enchanted limbo that would never end. Travel was, after all, so wonderfully thrilling, and if the distant future held the prospect of long tours with the Dominick Company it would be wholly satisfying.

Switzerland again! The country she had loved so much when she was twelve! The russet roofs of Berne, and then Thun and the dazzling blue waters of the big lake . . . the first glimpse of the snow-peaks, the unbelievably perfect frieze made by the Eiger, the

Mönch and the Jungfrau against the clear sky. Drina stood out in the corridor and stared until her eyes ached. There was nothing in the world quite like mountains.

Then the train was spiralling up the steep precipices on one side of the grey-green River Kander and, by craning forward as the train shot out of one of the many tunnels, she was just able to glimpse a white shoulder of the Doldenhorn above.

At last they entered the deep and beautiful valley where Kandersteg stretched under the pine-woods, the stark rocks of the Löhner and the snowy pinnacles of the Blümlisalp and the Doldenhorn. The train stopped at the sun-drenched little station, where people were drinking wine and coffee under trailing vines, not, apparently, finding the arrival of an international train in the least surprising. And Drina looked out at the village she had loved so much, remembering the walks and climbs, the bright and friendly village street, the sound of cowbells in the flowery meadows.

She would have given much to leave the train and wander by that swift river – such a strange colour because it flowed from a glacier – past the old chalets with painted shutters, red roofs and colourful window-boxes.

But, after all, there was the thrill of the Lötschberg Tunnel and the Rhône Valley far below on the other side. She had never been that way, though she had thought often of what lay beyond the Alpine wall. She had thought often of Italy, thinking that she would one day go there for a holiday with her grandparents. Never, never with strangers, to face unknown relatives!

But she had almost given up fearing the meeting as the train roared out of the long tunnel and she very

soon saw the stark drop so close to the carriage wheels.
The Rhône Valley was so far below that it was almost
like being in an aeroplane.

Down and down and down they went at a great
speed, never more than a few feet from the precipice,
and Drina stood near an open window, with her hair
blowing, singing under her breath.

Later came the Simplon Tunnel, so black, hot and
noisy, and then, incredibly, they were in Italy and
everything was miraculously changed. Peeling pink
and yellow-washed houses instead of trim wooden
chalets, vines growing on stony, terraced hillsides,
dark, shabby children waving to the train.

"Italy!" thought Drina and felt her spine creep with a
sharp, nameless excitement. "Italy and I half-belong,
however astonishing it seems!" And at Domodossola
she leaned out into the quite hot sunshine, listening to
the Italian voices of the guards who were standing by
the doors while customs and passport officials came
along the train, watching their faces, breathing the
atmosphere of a strange country, trying to convince
herself that she was not dreaming.

"And to think I might have been a hopeless coward
and not come!" she thought, no longer envying Jenny
her holiday in the Warwickshire countryside.

They were having lunch when the train approached
the northern reaches of Lake Maggiore and, though the
food was so strange and delightful, Drina could
scarcely bring herself to eat. It was so beautiful . . . like
nothing she had ever seen before. Blue water, a blaze
of blossoming trees, pink and yellow and white villas,
with exotic gardens that went down to the lake, bright
boats . . .

"Oh, those islands!" she cried, for they were like

something out of a dream, floating on the still water, the largest one crowned with a palace or a castle.

"The Borromean Islands," said Signora Carletti, much pleased with her delight. "That is Isola Bella."

"It *is* beautiful!" said Drina and felt as though she had lost something lovely and strange when the lake was left behind and they were flying across the plain towards Milan.

Before she expected it they were in a great station, and at last she remembered all her shyness and uneasiness. Soon now the unknown grandmother. The unknown city.

BOOK TWO
Ballet in Italy

1

Drina in Milan

Signor Carletti secured a porter without difficulty and Drina followed rather slowly up the platform to the barrier. The sound of the Italian language was in her ears and she was suddenly deeply thankful that it was not altogether strange to her.

Signor Carletti had told her that they were to meet her grandmother by the enquiry bureau and they set off to walk along a vast hall. There were a great many little shops and stalls and Drina was fascinated by the things on sale – Italian books and magazines, brilliant postcards, exotic-looking packets of sweets and bottles of wine in raffia cases. There were innumerable coloured posters, too, and she was quite startled to see some advertising Britain.

In the fascination of the huge station she slightly forgot her uneasiness again, but her heart leaped when Signora Carletti cried, "There is your grandmother, Drina!"

Drina looked wildly through the milling crowd and at first her gaze fastened on a small, shrunken woman in heavy black. But then she realized that her companions were leading her towards a woman who did not look old at all, for her silver hair was smartly dressed and she was slim and tall; she wore a very smart outfit and what looked remarkably like a Paris hat. Mrs Chester dressed well, but not as smartly as that.

The shock was so great – for Drina had definitely been imagining a stiff, prim elderly woman, more awe-inspiring than her English grandmother – that at first she could only gape. But Signora Adamo did not seem to notice. She took Drina's hand in a perfectly gloved one and kissed her warmly on the cheek, while Drina noted in a dim way that the face under the smart hairstyle was gentle and kind.

"So you are here, at last! And not too tired after the so long journey, I hope?"

"No. I-I'm not tired at all, thank you. I enjoyed the journey."

"She was enchanted by the Alps and by our beautiful Lago Maggiore," said Signora Carletti.

"But the luggage? Has the child no luggage?"

Signor Carletti indicated the porter, who was waiting amiably at a slight distance.

"We may, perhaps, share a taxi?"

"But of course. It was most kind of you to bring Drina to Italy." The conversation was all in English, apparently in courtesy towards Drina. Signora Adamo turned to her granddaughter as they walked out of the great hall, between imposing pillars and down some steps.

"You speak no Italian, I suppose?"

"Yes, a little. I-I had an Italian friend at school and I also had some conversation lessons."

"How good! Mrs Chester did not explain that. It will be much help to you."

The taxi whirled them away round a huge square

with gardens and into the endless traffic of the city streets. The adults began to talk amongst themselves in Italian, but Drina did not attempt to listen. She was in Milan! And she had met her Italian grandmother. She stole a cautious look at the upright figure beside her, wondering how old she was. There were deep lines under the fine dark eyes, but otherwise she had a smooth pale complexion and was really exceedingly good-looking.

"At least she must have been when she was young," thought Drina. It was going to be very strange to live with someone almost unknown for nearly a fortnight, but it might be interesting, too.

The taxi turned into a quieter street and stopped before an enormous block of flats. There was a uniformed hall-porter in the doorway and he came forward to open the door. Drina said a hasty farewell to the Carlettis, thanking them for looking after her on the journey, and then pointed shyly to her cases.

In a moment they were crossing an imposing entrance hall and flying upwards in a lift. Floor after floor went by before it stopped and they stepped out into a wide quiet corridor.

"You also live in a block of flats, so I am told," said Signora Adamo as she took a key from her handbag. "Quite near to the Houses of Parliament and Westminster Abbey."

"Yes. They're quite modern, but not like this. Not so – so luxurious."

"I am most comfortable here. I live here since my husband – your grandfather – died some years ago. Being so high it is quieter. Our traffic –"

"I know." Drina had found the traffic almost frightening in the taxi, perhaps because of the fact that everything travelled on what was to her "the wrong side of the road".

"From your room you are able to see the Cathedral."

She ushered Drina into a small, rather plain room. There was a very modern picture of scarlet flowers against a curve of blue sea and, on the table near the bed, a vase filled with white roses.

"How lovely!" Drina cried, burying her nose in the flowers. Then she turned towards the window. Her gasp of pleasure made Signora Adamo smile. It was a very high window and she was able to see over, as well as between, the opposite buildings to the soaring pinnacles of the Cathedral. The sky was very, very blue, with an occasional dazzlingly white cloud.

"It's wonderful! I'm so glad I've got a view. I want to see the Cathedral properly as soon as I can. I often go into Westminster Abbey for a few minutes."

"It is very impressive," said her grandmother. "I remember your Abbey well, though it is some years since I was in London." Then she put out her hand and turned Drina round to face her. "Let me look at you, child! Yes, you have a look of the South. We are not really Northerners. You have inherited Nino's colouring – I always called your father Nino. But I thought the moment I saw you that you had something of your mother. The carriage of the head, yes. The way you walk, so like a true dancer."

Drina stood quietly under the two hands on her shoulders. "Did you – know my mother?"

"But of course. I saw her dance many times before my son married her. I was always most interested in the ballet. She danced perhaps once a year here in Milan and also in Rome. I used to visit Rome frequently and also Paris, where she danced fairly often. And then

Nino brought her to visit me. She was always so charming – I was very much attracted to her. It was a most bitter day when I learned that she was dead, and so soon after Nino himself."

"My father died of pneumonia?"

"Yes. He was not ever so strong. But Elizabeth –"

"Granny always calls her Betsy."

"To us she was Elizabeth. Now would you prefer to unpack first? Then a cup of tea? I am fond of tea in the English fashion."

"Yes, thank you. I shan't be very long." And Drina took her keys from her handbag and opened her larger case.

She was glad to be alone for a short while, and as she hurried about disposing of her clothes and other possessions she paused occasionally to look at those glorious pinnacles against the vivid sky.

At the bottom of the case were three pairs of ballet shoes and her practice costume. She looked at them a trifle doubtfully. Perhaps there would be no time for practising and yet she must fit it in if possible.

There was a fitted basin in a corner and she washed her hands and face, then combed her hair and went out rather shyly into the hall. The door of a big, bright room was open and she heard the chink of teacups.

"We could go down to the restaurant, but often I prefer to remain here. Sit in that chair by the window, my dear."

Drina watched her grandmother as she moved gracefully about.

"I never thought you'd speak such good English."

"I write it somewhat pedantically, and I am at the moment a little out of practice. But no doubt after a few days of your company I shall be colloquial again. When

I was young I was at school in Switzerland where there were many English girls and at one time I visited London fairly frequently. I often listen to English programmes on the radio and I read the English newspapers."

She handed Drina a cup of tea and offered a plate of delicious-looking little cakes.

"I hope, my dear, that it will not be dull for you. Just an old woman –"

"You don't look a bit old!" cried Drina and meant it.

"Well, I am fifty-seven next birthday, but people rarely believe me."

"And I couldn't be bored. Not seeing Italy for the first time and – and getting to know you."

Signora Adamo gave her a look that was almost shy.

"It is strange for both of us. You Nino's daughter, whom I saw only once when you were three months old. Such a very dark, pretty baby! I hope you will tell me about your London life?"

"Of course I will. *And* about Willerbury. I was eleven and three-quarters when we moved to London."

"I should like to hear it all. To be – brought up to date, does one say? No doubt you are going to be a great dancer, just like your mother."

Drina looked at her. "I don't know. No one can say. I'm just a junior at the Dominick Ballet School."

"And the Dominick Company comes to Milan next week. I have taken tickets, thinking you would wish to go."

Drina's eyes blazed. "Oh, how lovely! I never thought you would. To see them in Italy! What are the tickets for?"

"*Coppélia* and *Les Patineurs*. And another night for the new three-act ballet."

"*The Lonely Princess*? I went to the dress rehearsal. We all did. Oh, I'm so glad!"

Signora Adamo looked pleased. "It is well, then. And I thought perhaps I might ask Igor Dominick and perhaps Miss Volonaise and the present ballerina here for cocktails or a meal in the restaurant –"

"Oh, but –" Drina's heart gave a startled leap. "Oh, but you can't!"

"But certainly. I knew Igor Dominick's father, and also Igor Dominick himself when he was younger. Elizabeth, you see –"

Drina stared at her rather helplessly. She had never once thought of her Italian grandmother having any connection with the Dominick. It was a contingency that just hadn't occurred to her.

"But you really can't. They don't know – it's the greatest secret! You see –"

Signora Adamo recognised the distress in her voice and asked gently, "What is it I do not see, Drina?"

"They just don't *know*. About Elizabeth Ivory being my mother. To them I'm just a girl at the Dominick School. I didn't want them to know. When I went to the audition two years last January Granny didn't take me, in case anyone recognised her. I'm Drina Adams in London. They don't even know that my father was Italian."

"But why was that?"

"Because –" Drina gulped and almost prayed that she would understand. "Because my mother was so very famous and I – I wanted to succeed on my own. I didn't want to – to lean on her name. It's been hard, but it's still a secret. I want it to be until I prove myself – oh, please understand!"

Signora Adamo poured herself out a second cup of

tea. Her face was very thoughtful.

"I see. You show great strength of character. Very few girls –"

"I made up my mind on the night when I learned about my mother being Elizabeth Ivory. *I* didn't even know until I was twelve. Granny kept it from me. She never wanted Betsy to be a dancer and she always felt that she wouldn't have died but for that."

"Then we will keep it a secret if that is what you wish."

They were silent for a while, while Drina gazed out of the window at the whirling traffic below. Then Signora Adamo said, "Since you do not seem tired we will take a short walk. There will be no need for a coat, as the weather is unusually warm. We have had a mild winter and spring came early."

Drina leaped up eagerly and a few minutes later they were in the lift.

Drina was never to forget that first sight of the great Piazza del Duomo. For several moments she simply stood and gaped, with some of the hundreds of pigeons gathered about her feet. The crowds of people enjoying the warm sunshine, the sound of Italian on every hand, the impressive façade of the Cathedral, the pinnacles and statues soaring up into the sky . . . All took her breath away. Apart from London, she had seen few cities and the noise, the slightly alien atmosphere, the huge buildings all around, were quite a shock. But it was a pleasant, even an exciting, shock.

She and her grandmother stood for some time examining the great bronze door of the Cathedral, and then entered the vast building where the sunlight streamed through stained glass windows and candles flickered before many an ornate altar. The whole place was much too big for Drina to get more than a general impression on that first visit, but she certainly intended to get to know it better.

The sunlight seemed brighter than ever as they left the Cathedral and, crossing the road, approached the Galleria Vittorio Emanuele. In the Galleria were restaurants, with tables outside, and many fascinating shops.

"It's marvellous!" Drina cried, more than once. "So high! And oh! I do love the shops!"

She bought several wonderful postcards and some Italian stamps, so that she could write to her grandparents and Rose, Jenny and Ilonka that very evening, and she stood entranced before the clothes and the swathes of brilliantly coloured Italian silk in many windows.

"That lovely scarlet blouse! And that turquoise blue dress! I do so love bright colours." And Signora Adamo smiled approvingly and vowed to herself that before Drina left Milan she would have some new blouses and dresses.

In the Piazza alla Scala Drina gazed with awe at the frontage of the famous opera house and it was strange and thrilling to see the great posters advertising the Dominick Ballet Company.

Altogether it had been a most exciting day and already it seemed to have lasted for a long time. Was it really only that morning that she had seen the russet roofs of Berne and the River Kander tumbling down from the heights?

She would never have admitted it, but suddenly weariness was making her eyes prick and her legs ache. Signora Adamo glanced at her once or twice as they retraced their steps along the Galleria, and in the Piazza del Duomo she hailed a taxi and they were driven back to the block of flats.

"To bed, I think, very early," she said firmly and Drina didn't argue. During their early dinner in the restaurant she found herself blinking and having to stifle her yawns.

A telegram had been sent to the Chesters announcing her safe arrival, so not even one postcard was written that night. She was asleep almost as soon as her head touched the pillow.

2

The Dominick
in Italy

After two or three days in Milan Drina felt quite at home in the flat and was getting more and more confident over speaking the Italian language. A few people spoke a little English, but on the whole she heard nothing but Italian.

She and her grandmother were soon quite at ease together and both enjoyed the exchange of experiences. Drina heard all about Signora Adamo's youth on the coast near Rome, schooldays in Switzerland, her early marriage and about her children when they were young. Drina especially appreciated, naturally, stories about her father and for the first time he began to seem a real person. In her turn she told about the Willerbury days, the friendship with Jenny Pilgrim and her first dancing lessons. Unconsciously she also gave a picture of her English grandparents that Signora Adamo found very interesting and illuminating. She still nursed a slight feeling of bitterness that she had lost that long-ago battle for her son's child, and Drina's very vivid picture of Mrs Chester's character fitted in almost too well with her own conception of the Englishwoman she had never met. But patently Drina was fond of her grandmother, and did not resent that strength of character and the unyielding opinions that had made it necessary for her to have to fight for her dancing. Clearly it had been a difficult struggle, but over that, at least, Drina had won, even as a young child.

Mrs Chester sounded an excellent woman, but decidedly lacking in imagination. But, on the whole, she had made Drina happy and perhaps strengthened her. Sensitive and imaginative herself, Signora Adamo saw that Drina had the artist's temperament and had never found life easy. Perhaps she never would find it easy, and therefore possibly it was as well that she had behind her the practical commonsense of her English grandmother. All the same, Signora Adamo sighed occasionally, thinking how different her own life might have been if she had been able to take Drina as a baby.

Still, all that was long ago and it now seemed that she and Drina could be friends.

In her turn Drina liked her grandmother and found her company surprisingly interesting. She was a well-read woman who had travelled fairly widely and enjoyed the arts. She was certainly not ignorant of ballet, though opera was her great passion, not perhaps surprising with La Scala scarcely half a mile away.

On her third evening in Milan Drina wrote to Jenny.

Dearest Jenny,
I hope you got the card of the Galleria Vittorio Emanuele? It leads through from the Piazza del Duomo to the Piazza alla Scala and has lots of restaurants and shops. One shop sells the loveliest carved animals, and I bought a little deer for a sort of second mascot (Hansl being the first and altogether important one, and of course with me in Italy) and I've christened him Milano. I do love Milan, though it isn't really at all picturesque. It is huge and busy

and important-feeling, and I could sit in the Piazza del Duomo for hours and hours, just absorbing the foreign atmosphere and watching the people.

I love to walk in the public gardens and watch the children playing, and sometimes fighting. Most of them are very good-looking and, though some look terribly poor, they seem happy. I love the shops, too, and yesterday my Italian grandmother bought me a scarlet silk dress. She insisted, though I told her, most tactfully, that I had enough money to buy it myself. She says she hasn't had the pleasure of buying clothes for a young girl for a very long time. I think she has quite a lot of money, so I didn't worry about that. She says I can wear it the first time I go to see the Dominick. Yesterday, too, we went to Santa Maria delle Grazie to see da Vinci's painting of The Last Supper. It is actually in the refectory next to the church. It was quite strange to see it in reality, after being familiar with it for so many years.

We also went to the cinema yesterday evening (what a crowded day!) to see a new Italian film. I thought it really good.

You should hear me speaking Italian! I still do it rather slowly, and if I get flustered it all goes, but I understand people quite well.

Italian Granny (I never quite know what to call her, so mostly don't call her anything) is really nice. She wears very attractive clothes from Rome or Paris and doesn't look a bit old. We get on very well, and we have a good deal in common, but I don't really feel that she is a relation, not in the way that Granny at home belongs to me. It's rather a strange situation, I suppose, for both of us.

I sometimes feel rather odd, remembering that, if things had gone differently, I might have grown up here – entirely Italian. Think if I'd never known Willerbury, or *the old Grand Theatre, the Selswick School and you! Not to mention the Dominick. It could so easily have happened, too, if it hadn't been for the fight that Granny put up. I'm glad she did, but I think it made my Italian grandmother sad. She hasn't said much, but I'm sure she minded. I think there is a Ballet School attached to La Scala; I wonder if I should have gone to that?*

Italian food is great fun and mostly absolutely delicious. Granny said it would be oily, but it isn't. I'm getting quite clever with the menu and know more or less what things are now. One puts cheese on soup, and the veal is heaven, sometimes cooked in wine. Granny said she hoped I wouldn't be influenced to drink wine, but everyone takes it for granted here and I have had a little white wine. Chianti is dreadfully sour, but some of the others are nice.

Do write and tell me about the farm and I'll write again and tell you all that happens, especially when the Company arrives. Next week, perhaps, we are hiring a car and going to Stresa or Baveno and Lake Maggiore. I had just a glimpse from the train and it looked perfectly beautiful. We may go to Como, too. Life certainly isn't dull.

I really do long to hear from you.
> *Love from*
> *Drina.*

Drina had scarcely posted Jenny's letter when a card arrived from the farm in Warwickshire.

Shall be thinking of you going all Italian, but don't alter too much. The farm is great, as usual, and Esmeralda is splendid. A most handsome cat! I was in Stratford yesterday and remembered last Easter when we went to The Dream and you were so thrilled. But nothing drew me this time. It was King John. Love, Jenny.

The next morning there was quite a long letter from Ilonka. She now wrote English with some fluency and had a vivid pen. She, it seemed, was discovering England, rather as Drina was discovering Italy.

Mother has some holiday, she wrote, and yesterday we both went to see Sussex. We had a most wonderful, beautiful day on the Downs – so warm and still, and little flowers in the very short grass and the Channel so blue not far away. When first I came to England I was glad to be in a free country but I could not like the look of it, except just once or twice – the Houses of Parliament from across the river and snow in St. James's Park. But now I see another England: in the springtime. We had tea in Lewes, such an extremely historic town. I liked the Museum and the Castle. Tomorrow we are going to your Chiltern Hills that you love so much. Mother tells me that they are in places just a little like Sussex, with the same flint buildings and some open downland, but mostly it is beechwoods.

Terza is most busy preparing herself for the long tour. They leave for Italy on Friday and expect to reach Milan on Saturday afternoon at 2.30. I have told her to look out for you. Diary of a Dancer is making very much money and is to be translated into French, German, Dutch, Swedish and several other languages. Terza says that she feels now that she did not write it. When she sees it in bookshops it is some other person's book. She has many letters from all over the world and is kept busy answering all of them.

I wish you a very happy holiday.

With love from,
Ilonka.

And by the same post came a letter from Rose.

Dear Drina,

How I envy you in Milan. I suppose it's horrid of me, but home feels so small and cramping after Chalk Green Manor. My room is so small that I want to push out the walls, and I do miss the country so. It wouldn't be so bad if I were back at the Dominick, as I shall be by next year, I suppose, but in holiday time London seems stuffy and noisy. I took the boys to the Zoo yesterday, though it costs such a dreadful lot. That, I'm afraid, is the poor kids' holiday treat.

I'm reading a lot and trying to practise as best I can, but there really isn't space. I keep on thinking of the woods and the beech leaves unfurling, and being on Wain Hill with Petrouchka.

Of course I have to keep it all from Dad and Mum. They would be so hurt. Mum always wanted me to be a dancer, and she is proud of me, I think, but she did say once that she hoped being at Chalk Green wouldn't make too much of a lady of me, being with rich children, and she said she didn't know what she'd do if I got dissatisfied with home. I'm not dissatisfied, really – I love them all very much, but I do feel overcrowded and there doesn't seem much to do. The other day I walked over Hampstead Heath and went to Kenwood House. I kept on thinking of you, because I've never been there alone before. I met Daphne Daniety on the way back, out with Queenie and someone I think must have been Queenie's mother – the great Beryl Bertram? Anyway, she looks quite ordinary now, in a tweed coat and with faded hair. Catty of me? I expect so.

D. and Q. both gave me sickly grins, but didn't say anything. What a standoffish pair they are!

Oh, well, the holidays will pass and then comes a summer at Chalk Green again. I do look forward to it, but wish you were likely to be with me. Think of Lodge Hill on

*a hot afternoon, with our noses in the thyme and
candytuft.*

Love,
Rose.

"You seem to have plenty of friends," remarked
Signora Adamo, as Drina folded Rose's letter, and her
granddaughter laughed.

"Three very good friends. And so different. Isn't it
fun getting letters?"

One other letter was from Mrs Chester. She wrote:

My Dear Drina,

*I was relieved to receive the telegram announcing your
safe arrival. I trust that you were not too tired after the
journey and that you found Signora Adamo well.*

*I wonder how warm it is in Italy? Here the sun is
shining every day and the flowers in the parks are a
wonderful sight. Your grandfather took me up to Regent's
Park the other evening and the trees were a picture.*

*Take great care and keep your eyes on the traffic. It is
sure to be considerable in Milan. And watch what you eat;
I never trust foreign food, though I must admit that I
enjoyed the Swiss menus. Eat sparingly of strange dishes
and I should steer clear of 'sea food' in Genoa. I don't want
to hear that you are suffering from food poisoning, though
I know that many people thoroughly enjoy such dishes.*

*We are very well, but of course miss you. Grandfather
sends his love.*

Yours affectionately,
Granny.

Drina smiled rather wryly over the few rather
terse, unemotional sentences. How very like her
grandmother it was, and for that very reason,

presumably, the almost cold words induced in her a sudden, almost unbearable feeling of homesickness. She looked round the subtly foreign room and then over the roof-tops of Milan, fighting the tears that threatened to fill her eyes.

But she soon managed to overcome her emotion and it was shortly afterwards that Signora Adamo said, "It's such a very beautiful day that I think I shall telephone for a car to take us to Como. You would like that?"

"I'd love it!" Drina cried, for blue lake water and perhaps vine-covered hills would be better than hot city streets, however interesting.

At first the country was very flat, but Drina did not find it dull because the whole appearance of the land and the villages was so different from England. She was always intrigued by the lively, shabby groups of children and was relieved to realise that, even when patently poverty-stricken, they seemed happy. The faces of the old men and women fascinated her, too, and once, after passing a group of black-clad crones sitting outside one of the ancient, peeling houses she said:

"Sometimes I wish that I could paint or draw. No wonder Italy has produced so many great artists!"

"To dance is your art," said her grandmother, sitting back comfortably in the big, smoothly-running car.

"I know. I shall have to learn to interpret life through that. But so many of these faces and buildings make me want to catch them and hold them. Make other people see them."

In the April sunshine the lakeside at Como looked very colourful. The Piazza Cavour was bright with flowers and people sat drinking coffee and wine outside the restaurants. There were brilliantly coloured boats in the harbour, as well as some small steamers, and Drina's eyes were very busy taking it all in – including the hills about the lake.

Signora Adamo greatly preferred the modern shops in the newer part of the town, but, after they had looked at the rather dark and gloomy Cathedral, Drina led her into the ancient, much narrower streets. They were a trifle smelly in parts, but infinitely more interesting to the girl from England.

They had lunch in the open air, since Drina begged so eagerly not to go indoors, but Signora Adamo remarked that, in spite of the unusual warmth of the sun, the season was very far from having started. To Drina it was warm enough to bathe, but she noticed that it seemed mostly to be the foreign visitors who wore the lightest clothes. The ones who were obviously Italian still wore garments that were decidedly unsummery. For herself she was extremely hot and did not even need to wear her jacket.

Later Signora Adamo suggested a short sail on the lake and Drina was delighted. She stood in the bow of the steamer, with her hair blowing in the warm wind, her eyes dazzled by the reflections from the blue water. The steamer called in at Cernobbio, a small village with trees close to the water, and then went on again giving many glimpses of palatial villas in wonderful gardens filled with exotic flowering trees.

Drina was sorry when they were nearing Como again and for the first time she began to look forward to going to Genoa. Milan was interesting, but it would be delightful to be by the Mediterranean, perhaps idling by one of those picturesque harbours that Emilia had described.

She hurried cheerfully off the steamer and was much

startled when she heard a cry of pain behind her. When she swung round, her grandmother was clutching the side of the little gangway, her face white with pain.

"My foot! I stumbled and twisted my ankle!"

Immediately a sympathetic crowd began to gather, everyone talking in Italian, and one of the sailors helped Signora Adamo to a seat on the promenade. Drina hovered anxiously, and Signora Adamo caught her eye and said quickly:

"I think I see our car along there. Please summon the driver, Drina."

"But – but oughtn't you perhaps go to an hotel and rest?"

"No. I should prefer to get home. Hurry, Drina, my dear."

Fortunately the driver was sitting in the car, reading a newspaper, and within a minute or two Signora Adamo was settled on the back seat, with her already swollen foot on a cushion. Drina sat in the front and they were watched on their way by the remaining members of the little crowd.

"Such a nuisance!" Signora Adamo said. "This ankle is a trifle weak. I sprained it badly last year. I fear it will mean resting it for a day or two."

Her doctor, who arrived half an hour after they reached the flat, agreed emphatically.

"But of course you must rest," he said in Italian. "There can be no question of walking on that foot, not even to the lift, until at least the day after tomorrow. Meals can be brought up? That's all right, then. And no doubt the young visitor can amuse herself?"

"I shall be all right," Drina said shyly in the same language.

"She must never go out alone, though," her grandmother said anxiously. "It wouldn't be suitable."

Drina held her peace for the time being. It seemed to her that she would be perfectly all right alone, even in a foreign city. She knew her way about now, helped by the study of a good street map, and could not get lost. Years of walking about London alone had made her thoroughly independent.

She contented herself with practising, trying to read Italian magazines, listening to the radio and talking to her grandmother, but by the next afternoon – Saturday – she longed to be out.

After lunch she began a cautious attack.

"Don't you think I might go out for a little while? Honestly, I won't talk to strangers and I shan't get lost or run over. I'm used to London and –"

Her grandmother looked at her worriedly. She was still suffering pain from her foot and a rest would be welcome.

"But, child, I hardly think that Mrs Chester would like it. In Italy –"

"She won't know," Drina said wickedly. "Or not until I'm safely back in London. And there's something I really want to do."

"What is that?"

"I want to go to the station and see if the Dominick Company arrives safely."

"Very well. I will telephone for a taxi –"

"I can walk, truly. It isn't far and I know the way. And I love stations. At home I sometimes go into Victoria Station to watch the boat trains leave."

Her grandmother gave in and Drina flew into her room to tidy her hair, wash her hands and find her shoulder-bag. She went down in the lift and was warmly greeted by the hall porter, who had daughters of his own and was interested in Signora Adamo's English granddaughter.

"She moves most beautifully," he had told his wife, only the previous evening. "A dancer, I am told. One can easily see that she must be good."

Drina enquired after Giovanna, Lucia and Ginevra and then smiled and stepped briskly out into the bright sunshine. It was exciting and satisfying to be alone at last and she hoped that people would take her for an Italian girl walking her native city.

It seemed that to foreigners, at least, she must look confident, for, waiting to cross the great square by the station, she was addressed by a bewildered-looking little party of three middle-aged women. She had decided that they were probably English before they spoke a word.

"*Scusi, Signorina!* Er – what's the Italian for 'Cathedral', Maud, dear? *El Duomo, Signorina?* We wish –"

Drina laughed.

"It's all right. I'm English."

"What a relief! There was such a crowd at the enquiry place at the station, but no one else speaks a word of English, so it seems. We've come from Lugano for the afternoon."

Drina gave quick, clear instructions and watched their relieved faces with some amusement. Yes, it was pleasant to feel even a little at home in a foreign city.

She crossed to the station cheerfully, one hand on her shoulder-bag, and passed through its vast impressive portals. Twenty past two! Well, there was plenty to look at until the train arrived. She walked the length of the huge hall slowly, stopping to buy postcards, stamps and a packet of sweets. Already the handling of *lire* was becoming quite easy.

A man at the enquiry office told her that the train was twenty minutes late and what platform it would arrive at, and presently she established herself a little way from the barrier. Standing there, with the crowds whirling past her and snatches of many languages in her ears, she was suddenly visited by a feeling of utter incredulity.

Drina Adams all alone in the Stazione Centrale in Milan! Drina Adams waiting to see the Dominick Ballet Company arrive in Italy!

"I don't feel in the least like me," she thought.

At last the great electric engine slid to a standstill and people began to pour out on to the platform. Drina stood on tiptoe, craning her neck. The first person she picked out was Catherine Colby herself, looking as elegant as if she had not just had a long journey. Her fair hair was beautifully set and she wore a black suit with a short, fluffy pale coat over it. With her were Peter Bernoise and two of the most important soloists. They were giving orders to a porter and then turning to laugh amongst themselves. Someone with a news camera appeared out of the surging crowd and they turned round, still laughing, to pose for photographs.

The members of the *corps de ballet* appeared more slowly. Some of them looked tired and untidy, but all were smiling. Drina knew most of them by name now, in company with nearly every other pupil in the School. Suddenly she sighted Bettina Moore, very young and pretty, and behind her Terza Lorencz, wearing a blue coat.

Igor Dominick had joined the little group that was talking to the reporter, and with him a familiar, elegant figure – Marianne Volonaise.

Suddenly Drina gave a little gasp, for the young Igor Dominick was there, too, wearing a pale-coloured anorak and, as she had usually seen him, looking remote and rather bored. He was carrying a shabby suitcase with many foreign labels and there was a bundle of illustrated papers under his arm. One of the youngest members of the *corps de ballet* spoke to him and he shrugged and raised his eyebrows in that rather supercilious way he had, though Drina had long ago decided that he was all poses and probably lonely and not too happy underneath. How could anyone be happy, even with a father so important as Igor Dominick, when he had no friends?

Most of the travellers were off the train by now and the dancers were moving towards the barrier. Drina ducked behind a trolley laden with luggage, because she didn't particularly want to be seen. But Terza's quick eyes had spotted her and she came over, smiling.

"Oh, Drina, it *is* so nice to see you! You came especially to welcome us?"

"Just to make sure you'd all arrived safely," Drina said shyly.

"But yes. We arrived safely, all of us, and the scenery and costumes also, one hopes. Are you enjoying your holiday?"

"Oh, yes. And I'm coming to see you twice."

Terza flew off to join the others and Drina went to buy herself a fruit drink before walking back to the flat. Her cheeks were burning and she felt unexpectedly happy and elated.

The Dominick had arrived in Italy and on Monday she would see *Les Patineurs* and *Coppélia* at La Scala. Life was very satisfying and exciting.

3

In the Piazza
del Duomo

By Monday Signora Adamo's foot was strong enough
for her to be able to walk a little. She was able to
go down to the restaurant for meals, but she did not
feel like making any greater effort, not, at any rate,
until the evening. She was very distressed for Drina's
sake, but Drina told her not to worry.

She practised for some time in the big bathroom,
where there was a very suitable towel-rail that could act
as a *barre*, and then said that she would go for a short
walk, just as far as the Piazza del Duomo. Her
grandmother was still not very sure of the correctness
of letting Drina walk about Milan on her own, but she
had certainly returned from the station quite safely and
also from a Sunday stroll in the public gardens. So she
said:

"Very well, my dear. English girls, one realises, are
very independent, but I am thinking of Mrs Chester
and the fact that you are entrusted to me."

Drina laughed. "I'll be quite safe, honestly. I'll just
have another look at the Cathedral and buy some more
postcards. I'll be back in time for lunch."

She went off confidently, walking briskly towards
the Piazza del Duomo, and she entered the Cathedral

through the main door, becoming absorbed very quickly in the beauty and quiet and noticing, as she did at almost every turn in Italy, the aged faces before the flickering candles of many an altar. Her fingers itched for a pencil, though she was sadly aware that she had no great artistic talent. There was something about the expressions, the very bone structure, that made her long passionately to catch them with a few swift strokes.

The weather was still exceedingly warm for April and by the time Drina had lingered for a while in the centre of the Piazza near the equestrian statue, watching the passing scene, she was very hot and thirsty. Over on the south side of the square, under some cool-looking arches, were a few café tables, where people were drinking in a leisurely way. She waited for a lull in the traffic, crossed the road and seated herself at an unoccupied table.

The waiter was so little and dark that her mind immediately registered that he came from the far South. She ordered orangeade and, the moment it came, took a long, satisfying drink. Then, since the waiter had put down the bill she opened her shoulder-bag and groped for her purse.

The waiter was hovering beside her, waiting for the money, and Drina's blood suddenly seemed to run cold. Her groping fingers did not alight, as they usually automatically did, on her purse, and she opened the bag to its widest and began to search frantically amongst the contents – comb, handkerchief, keys, various letters, a little silk scarf carefully folded. There was no sign of her red purse and suddenly she remembered taking it out in her bedroom to count her *lire* notes. They generally got into a grubby bundle by the end of the day.

Evidently she had been thoroughly careless and left the purse on the table and she had not even her travellers' cheques with her, for she always left them at the flat.

The waiter's dark eyes were fixed on her unwaveringly and Drina felt a hot flush staining her face. She turned the bag out on the table, though she now knew quite well that the purse was not there. A few Italian coins of almost no value rolled across the table and tinkled on the flagstones and she looked after them in despair.

"I am so sorry, but I have left my purse at home," she said to the waiter in careful Italian, and he immediately began to talk very fast and very indignantly, so that people at other tables turned to stare.

Well, after all, she had not finished drinking the orangeade, but that would make no difference. Drina had visions of being led away to some frightening police station. The waiter certainly looked angry enough. He was saying something about "English visitors". How on earth did he *know* that she was English?

Suddenly a slightly foreign voice said at her elbow, "Perhaps I can assist you? You seem to be in trouble?"

Drina spun round and looked up into the face of the young Igor Dominick. She was certainly deeply glad to see him, but she wished heartily that he was not looking so amused and superior.

"Oh, yes. The waiter wants the money. And I've left my purse at home. If you could –"

He brought out a bundle of notes and handed the waiter a couple. The waiter looked at them carefully, as

though expecting to find something wrong with them, then nodded more amiably and went off to serve three Germans who were signalling impatiently.

Drina took a gulp of the orangeade – her throat had gone drier than ever with panic – and then looked across at Igor Dominick who had taken the opposite seat.

"Thank you very much. I'll let you have it back this afternoon. Perhaps I could give it to the doorkeeper at the theatre?"

He was eyeing her in a rather puzzled fashion.

"I do know you, don't I?"

Drina was still a trifle upset and something in his expression was very disconcerting.

"Well, you ought to. You've seen me off and on for three months," she said, with unusual asperity.

He was frowning, but she thought fleetingly that he was really very handsome. If only he would alter his manner and let himself be human he would be a different person.

"Oh, yes, I know! You're one of the little girls at the Dominick! Surely you're too young to be out alone in a foreign city?"

No girl of fourteen and a half likes to be called a "little girl" by a boy scarcely a year older, and Drina suddenly entirely forgot that she had always wanted to know Igor Dominick better. She heartily agreed with all the members of the School who had found him impossible.

She finished her drink at a gulp and sprang to her feet. Her eyes were blazing and her voice shook with temper, though she kept it very low.

"It may interest you to know that I shall be fifteen next autumn and that I'm perfectly capable of looking after myself. It was just an accident that I left my purse at home. I don't *wonder* you're unpopular at the Dominick! You do nothing but look amused and superior, and you don't even bother to find out about other people. I'm only one class below you, as you'd know if you gave it one moment's thought. In fact, you think far too much of yourself. I wish I hadn't needed to borrow a penny of your money!"

Igor Dominick looked at her with genuine astonishment. Drina's temper did not often flare out, but when it did she looked a different person: brilliant-cheeked, bright-eyed, her hair swinging back from her neat little ears.

"But, I say! Wait a minute –"

Drina, however, had gone, weaving her way through the tables. Someone was rising from the end table and Drina almost cannoned into her. She stopped abruptly, for it was Bettina Moore.

"Oh, I'm dreadfully sorry, Bettina!" she cried and then thought wildly that she should probably have said "Miss Moore". Only she had known Bettina for so long at a distance that she always thought in terms of Christian names. And, besides, Bettina still looked so very young, though she must be nearly nineteen. She had a very round, childish face and probably she, too, suffered much the same indignities that Drina had just experienced.

Bettina Moore grinned in a friendly way.

"Fancy seeing you here, Drina!"

Drina gaped at her. *She* had been aware of Bettina Moore ever since she had danced Little Clara in *Casse Noisette* while still a student at the Dominick School, but there was no reason on earth why Bettina Moore should know Drina Adams.

"How – how d'you know who I am?"

Bettina laughed and, taking her arm in a light grasp, turned to cross the road towards the wide space in the centre of the Piazza.

"Walk along with me, will you? I ought to go back. We're rehearsing like mad, but I wasn't needed for half an hour so I slipped out for some air and a drink. Why shouldn't I know you? I've often seen you about and I was at the matinée last December. I admired your Changeling very much."

"Oh!" Drina's temper had quite gone and she was beginning to be ashamed of herself. She nearly always was, afterwards.

"Besides, you had a touch of fame a year or two ago, didn't you?"

"Do you mean in *Argument*?" ⸱ ⸱

"Of course. It wasn't a good play, but your notices were all really good. You're not altogether an insignificant member of the School."

Drina laughed. "I am, you know. That was what I was so mad with Igor Dominick about. He just dimly knew he'd seen me somewhere and called me 'little girl'. I had to borrow some *lire* off him, too!"

Bettina stopped under the statue of Vittorio Emanuele and looked at her thoughtfully. She was taller than Drina, certainly, but not very much.

"I was just coming to your rescue when he got up from a nearer table. Poor kid, he's had a wretched time lately. I have tried to be friendly with him since we left London, but I'm afraid the rot's gone rather deep. He hates the Dominick. He never wanted to leave Paris in the first place. Mr Dominick is worried to death about him, I believe, though he doesn't say much. Not to me, anyway."

A feeling of guilt was rapidly taking possession of Drina.

"And I bit his head off! Oh, dear! But he *can* be so annoying. Everyone seems to find him so."

"They do, unfortunately. He started off on the wrong foot and he stayed wrong until the end of term. It's that half-amused, bored, remote, and supercilious manner."

"Yes, it is," Drina agreed. "Though I've always liked the look of him and been a bit curious. Only then he called me 'little girl' in such an 'I'm patting you on the head' sort of way and I flared up. I've got a dreadful temper, though it doesn't often get the better of me."

They set off again, across the second road and into the Galleria, and Bettina said slowly, "He does need a friend near his own age. Couldn't you – well, have another shot?"

"I haven't had one shot yet," Drina said ruefully.

"He's been motherless since he was a baby and the Paris aunt doesn't seem to have taken much interest in him. But he was happy in Paris, all the same, and I'm told he's a most promising dancer. Mr Dominick suddenly seems to have decided that he wanted him with him and that it was absurd that his own son wasn't at the Dominick. Why not come and watch the rehearsal now and perhaps he'll wander in?"

Drina was sorely tempted. It would be wonderful to sit in La Scala and watch the Company at work. But a glance at her watch told her that time had passed surprisingly quickly and that her grandmother would be worried if she were not back soon.

"I wish I could. But I've got to be back for lunch and my – the person whom I'm staying with doesn't really like me to be out alone."

"Someone said you had Italian relations?"

"Yes." It was awkward not to be able to explain that she had an Italian grandmother, but Drina was loathe to let anyone hear the name Adamo. There was always the possibility that it might be remembered that Elizabeth Ivory was really Elizabeth Adamo. "And I've got some more in Genoa. I'm going there on Friday."

Bettina laughed.

"Nice for you to have us around, isn't it? Well, look here! Could you be by that statue in the Piazza – the horse one – about eleven tomorrow morning? I'll have a tactful word with the lad and say *you're* lonely or something. If you don't mind, that is? But it will be better to let him think – well –"

"That he's benefiting *me*?" Drina said, a trifle wryly. "If he comes I'll say I'm sorry I exploded and I can give him the *lire* that I borrowed."

"It would be sporting of you, and he really is both nice and intelligent. Once or twice I've thought he could be really amusing."

At the end of the Galleria Drina said goodbye and turned on her heel. As she walked back to the block of flats she felt that it had been an eventful morning. First finding herself with no money, then the absurd little scene with Igor Dominick – she did wish very heartily that she had not lost her temper – and then the conversation with Bettina Moore. After more than two years of wanting to get to know someone it was odd that it should happen so casually in the Piazza del Duomo, Milan.

Signora Adamo had no intention of missing the opening night of the ballet, to Drina's acute relief. She had been afraid, at the back of her mind, that the ankle would still be too bad. Certainly she would not be allowed to go to the theatre all alone.

But when she arrived back from the two meetings in the Piazzo del Duomo, her grandmother was walking about with fair ease.

"We will have a taxi, of course, and I shall manage very well. Don't worry, Drina. You shall wear your new red dress and see all your friends dancing. You look very flushed, my dear!"

"I hurried," Drina explained and, over lunch, she told a little about Igor Dominick's son and how she was perhaps meeting him the following morning.

Her grandmother listened with much interest.

"Poor boy! And very good-looking, you say? Well, never fear, he will not be long without friends. Good-looking young men never are, and if he is intelligent also – would you perhaps like to invite him to accompany us to Stresa on Wednesday?"

Drina hesitated, her knife and fork hovering over the delicious salad.

"I don't even know if he'll come in the morning. And, you see, I can't ask him because of – I told you – no one must know about Mother."

Signora Adamo sighed. She did not wholly approve of Drina's fixed intention of keeping the secret. It was no use arguing, of course, and it certainly showed great character to wish to succeed without the aid of a famous mother, but still –

"I might perhaps have another name for the day. It would be dishonest, but if you feel you would like to ask the boy I could perhaps be your Aunt Andrina. Or 'great aunt' might be rather more suitable. But one day you will find yourself in – how do you say? A muddle?"

"Yes, I can see that I may," Drina agreed. "Oh, but it is terribly nice of you! Still, I don't suppose he'll come."

"Except perhaps to get his money," she added to herself, for she had not told that part of the story, not wishing to upset her grandmother.

She thought a good deal about Bettina Moore and young Igor Dominick during the afternoon, but, as evening drew on, everything was superseded by excitement. It was thrilling to put on the new scarlet silk dress and Signora Adamo produced a delicate silver necklace and earrings to match.

"A present for you, Drina dear. You have such pretty ears. Ah, yes, they suit you very well."

Drina had never worn earrings before, but it was true that they suited her remarkably well.

With her soft white cape round her shoulders she certainly looked more grown up than usual and she found herself wishing fleetingly that Igor Dominick could see her.

Staring at herself in the looking-glass she thought, with triumph and a strange regret, "I *am* small, but I'm growing up, all the same. I want to, and yet I don't want to. I want to hold time back and yet rush on. Oh, dear! Perhaps I don't really know what I want!"

One thing was certain, however. The evening was one of extraordinary happiness, so wonderful that she had no words to express her feelings when at last it was over.

To sit in one of the most famous opera houses in the world, amidst a cheerful and glittering throng of people, was exciting enough. But to add to everything it seemed to Drina that the Dominick Company took on a special magic that night. She loved *Coppélia* and had thought that she knew it well, but the ballet seemed in every way more enchanting. New sets and costumes had been designed for the European tour and the colours were glorious, the music carried Drina away on waves of rhythm and sweeping sound, so that she could not keep her feet quite still, and Catherine Colby's Swanilda was altogether delightful.

She always loved the first act especially, with its mazurka and czardas, and she particularly liked the music in the second act to which the mechanical dolls came to life. The third act, with its Masque of the Hours, was delightful, too, and towards the end of the ballet that strange experience that sometimes came to Drina held her in an unusual grip, so that for minutes on end she really seemed to be on the great stage, one with the dancers.

She sat in a daze when the curtain came sweeping down and then rose again on the assembled company, and Signora Adamo looked at her almost anxiously. The child was undoubtedly an artist; it was clearly seen that she passionately loved the ballet. No doubt one day –

"One day," she said, when the curtain fell for the last time, "perhaps you will dance Swanilda here." And she was quite startled by the passion with which Drina replied:

"I hope I will! Oh, if only I could know that I'll be a ballerina!" And then, much more quietly: "But it would be enough just to dance here. Just to be in the *corps de ballet*."

"I think," said her grandmother, as they left their seats, "that you will go further than that."

4

Making Friends

The next morning Signora Adamo had a letter from her daughter Giulia Gardino, saying that she, her husband and her daughter Antonia were all looking forward to meeting Drina.

"She also says," Signora Adamo explained, "that she has done as I suggested and got tickets for the ballet. Antonia is exceedingly fond of ballet and much envies you because you train for the life. You will like Giulia, and her husband is a charming man. He works in one of the Government offices in Genoa, in one of the fine buildings that was once a palace."

"I want to see Antonia," Drina remarked.

"She is a pretty girl – not so dark as you. And clever, I believe."

That morning, also, Drina had a letter from Emilia, now at her home in Genoa.

Dear Drina (wrote Emilia in her fluent English),
It will be fun to see you. Do telephone as soon as you arrive and perhaps we can arrange something. I long to help to show you our beautiful city.

How much do you like Milano? I wonder if you've been to see the Dominick yet? The tickets have sold very rapidly

*here, but Mother managed to get some. I said I just had to
see them in Italy. I never have before. When they've come
I've been at Chalk Green.*

*Yesterday I went to Camogli to visit some family friends
who have a sailing boat. The sun was really hot and the
water so calm and blue. I thought of you and how much
you would like the harbour and the coloured villas and the
olive groves on the hills. We sailed round the promontory
into the deep rocky harbour of San Fruttuoso, and then on
to Portofino, where we had a meal.*

*We live in a flat, and have no garden, but I have seen
here lilac and roses and also wallflowers and pansies. I
know you once said it was funny that we had 'English'
flowers. There is wistaria, too, beginning to hang in a
purple curtain, and chestnut trees in flower.*

*Chalk Green seems very far away and I expect London
does to you. I had a card from Hildegarde from Freiburg.
They are going to stay at Hinterzarten in the Black Forest
for a few days. Do you remember how she used to talk
about it all? And the twins sent a card from Jersey, where
they are on holiday.*

*Bianca loved Chalk Green and she says she is looking
forward to the summer term.*

We are both looking forward to seeing you.

Love from
Emilia.

*P.S. I had a card from Christine. Would you believe it? She
is in Paris again. Do you remember how she talked and
talked about it last year? I never shall like her!*

Drina went off to the Piazza del Duomo as she had
promised, but she had no real certainty that Igor
Dominick would be there, or, if there, that they would
manage to get on amicably.

She crossed the centre of the square rather slowly, her interest centred on the various foreigners drifting about in small and large parties. It always amused her to try and guess their nationalities before she heard them speak. It was a game that she had played very successfully in Switzerland, and it was just as much fun in Italy. Germans were generally easy to recognise, and so were French people, but she often thought English people Dutch and the other way round. Scandinavians were easy, too, and she rarely failed over Americans, who generally seemed to be in a hurry but desperately anxious not to miss anything.

She was puzzling over one little group of a father, mother and spectacled boy when she nearly cannoned into Igor Dominick, who was strolling towards her.

"Oh, hullo!" Drina recovered herself quickly and tried to smile in a really friendly way. "I was trying to decide what nationality those three are. I often try to guess."

"I can tell you that," the tall, dark boy said easily. "They're Belgian. I was sitting on a seat with them just now. And that other lot – the pretty girl in pink, do you see? – are from Vienna. One does see the world."

"I enjoy it," said Drina.

"Oh, so do I. I used to do it in Paris. The English were rarely attractive. As a nation they are not appealing."

Drina laughed, for he had so quickly gone back to his usual tone.

"But you're English yourself!"

"I was born in England; so was my father. But his family, as you probably know, were mainly Russian, and my mother was French. Bettina Moore says you're partly Italian. I find the Italians perhaps more appealing than any other race."

It seemed to be intended as a compliment and Drina dimpled. He was certainly in a good mood.

They were strolling across the square and stopped to watch some children feeding the pigeons. She groped in her shoulder-bag and held out some money.

"Thank you very much, and – and I'm sorry I lost my temper."

The dark eyes looked down at her.

"You did flare up. Still, I suppose I insulted you by thinking you only a little girl. Bettina says you had a part in a West End play and are a very promising dancer. I haven't got a tenth of the girls at the Dominick sorted out. I know Queenie Rothington – prominent teeth and a vast opinion of herself! – and that pretty one called Lorna. And the fair one who's growing too much. Daphne –"

Drina was staring at him with wide eyes.

"Queenie *has* prominent teeth, now you come to mention it, but I never thought about it before. I thought it was only *girls* who were supposed to be catty?"

"Don't you believe it," he said airily. "One notices things and one perhaps speaks of them."

"And Daphne – once she was terribly worried because she was growing rather fast, but then she stopped. Or I thought she had. How do you know –?"

"I overheard her speaking of it. She said she had grown an inch since Christmas."

"Oh, poor Daphne!" Drina cried, for the spectre of growing too much hung over so many of the pupils at the Dominick.

"She is a friend?"

"Oh – no. As a matter of fact she doesn't like me,

though we've known each other for years. But I hate to think that anyone's worried about growing."

"*You* at least, have no need to worry," he said, with a funny sidelong look that made Drina laugh again.

"Not if I can still be taken for a little girl!"

He said suddenly, "Shall we return to our café of yesterday and have drinks together? That will show I am forgiven, and it's so very hot."

Drina nodded and they crossed the road and settled themselves at a shady table.

He ordered fruit drinks and, when they came, began to talk again. Drina asked a question about the ballet school in Paris and he was soon well away, describing his life in France. He talked vividly and seemed almost a different boy from the one she had seen in the distance all the previous term. Gone was the unnatural, irritating manner and she thought fleetingly that if the others could see and hear him they would not dislike him so much.

Presently he went on to talk about his rather abrupt transfer to his father's London house, where a housekeeper was in charge.

"I didn't wish to go, though I admire my father. The Dominick is a good school – the best in England, except perhaps for the Royal Ballet School – but for myself I prefer to live in Paris."

"But couldn't you – er – try to settle down? Since you *have* to be there, I mean."

He was staring at the passing traffic.

"I suppose I shall have to. But now one has made oneself unpopular –"

"You did make them cross," Drina said frankly. "They thought you dreadfully superior and critical and they didn't like it. But – but –"

"If I were to be my natural sweet self?" he countered, suddenly grinning in a very likeable way.

"Yes. Something like that."

"Perhaps you don't know how very difficult it is, when one has started in a certain way –"

"I do," Drina said eagerly. "I was taken away from the Dominick in London and sent to Chalk Green in the country. I loathed it at first and I couldn't do anything right. They were almost the worst months of my life. But then I got to like it and I learned a lot from the change –" She hesitated, not wanting it to seem that she was preaching.

"No doubt you're right," he agreed. "And since I'm to be at the Dominick now until I join the Company I had far better learn to like it. You see, I've been thinking things out since reaching Italy."

"I'm glad," Drina said frankly. "After all, you *are* Mr Dominick's son and we all look up to him dreadfully. It must be very – very odd for you. I suppose you know everyone, and –"

"Marianne Volonaise is my godmother," he said. "And when she was first married my mother entertained all the great ones of the ballet world. But she died when I was three and since then I've been much alone. At first with a French nurse, you see, and then, when I was old enough to dance, that filled my life. That, and Paris. I'm used to being much alone, but still –"

He talked on, giving, perhaps unconsciously, a very clear picture of the rather lonely boy who had learned to know Paris and to whom dancing had taken the place of most other things.

Drina was quite startled when she looked at her watch and saw how time had passed.

"I must go! Really I must. My – my aunt will be worrying." Suddenly shy again, she eyed the boy opposite rather doubtfully. "I suppose you wouldn't – that is, we're hiring a car tomorrow and going to Stresa. If you'd like to come –"

Rather to her surprise he said quite promptly, "That's very kind. Milan is so hot, noisy and dusty. I should like to go if your aunt wouldn't mind."

"She asked me to ask you." Drina felt guilty about the deception, but Igor Dominick was clearly the last person who could be allowed to know that she had a grandmother whose name was Adamo. He obviously had a well-stocked mind and might know a lot about Elizabeth Ivory.

Drina asked the name of his hotel and said that they would pick him up the following morning.

"But we have to be back for the evening performance. I don't want to miss *The Lonely Princess*."

He walked most of the way with her towards the flat and then saluted and turned back. Drina entered the cool entrance hall, her mind filled with the pictures he had conjured up.

"I do like him," she told herself. "He seems to have had a strange life and rather a sad one. If we saw much of each other I think we might quarrel occasionally, but he isn't dull. Now Jan Williams is always nice and kind, but he *is* a bit dull."

The dark and unusually serious face of young Igor Dominick came back to her several times during the afternoon and evening, and she wrote a long letter to Rose, telling her about the two meetings in the Piazza.

I really think I shall like him, she finished. *Anyway, I shall know better after tomorrow. Oh, Rose, I wish you were here and could come to Stresa, too.*

The trip to Stresa was certainly a success. The sun shone once again in a dark blue sky and it was good to leave the city. Igor Dominick made himself very agreeable to Signora Adamo and she seemed to like him. He called her simply "Madame" and did not seem to notice that she had not been given a surname.

Drina listened to their conversation and joined in occasionally, but a good deal of her attention was given to the passing scene. She was very thrilled when they came in sight of the vast lake, so bright and still between the mountains. The villas dreamed in the sun and there were flowering trees everywhere.

"Oh, the boats! And those islands! And those high, high mountains in the distance! I wish I could sail away right up the lake. Where would I get to?"

"It is a very long lake," said her grandmother, "and would take several hours. In the end you would reach Switzerland – Ascona, Locarno, Maggadino."

"I row very well," Igor Dominick remarked. "We might perhaps go on the lake after lunch?"

"You shall take Drina while I rest," Signora Adamo said. "But remember that we must leave in good time for the ballet."

They reached Stresa earlier than they had expected, so Signora Adamo decided that they would all go over to Isola Bella in one of the launches, see the island and the palace, and return to one of the big hotels by the quay for lunch. It was still so early in the season that the crowds were not very great and, besides themselves, there were only two small parties in the boat: a German family and half a dozen young French people.

Drina stood near the bow, lost in enchantment. It was so beautiful . . . in some ways the most beautiful place she had ever seen in her life. The bright water . . . the island they were approaching, with its terraces and statues and flowering trees . . . the distant snow-peaks on the horizon . . . the villas on the mainland shores . . . the touch of the sun on her neck and bare arms. It was perfect! A dream place. She thought briefly of Rose in the stuffy little house at Earl's Court and felt deeply thankful for her own good fortune. There were plenty of other girls at the Dominick who rarely had more than a day by the sea.

"And to think I didn't want to come to Italy!" she said aloud, then found Igor Dominick at her side.

"You didn't wish to come?"

"No. I – I was shy of my Italian relations and I wanted to go and stay in Warwickshire with my friend Jenny Pilgrim."

"She dances also?"

"No, she doesn't. She wants to be a farmer," Drina said, a trifle mischievously, and saw the well-marked eyebrows go up in real or pretended disgust.

"Ugh! I find farms smelly and unpleasing. In France –"

"They do smell," Drina agreed cheerfully. "But Jenny doesn't mind and neither do I now. But I am so glad that I came to Italy!"

Drina followed the others through the impressive rooms of the palace, but it was the gardens that drew her. They were laid out in ten artificial terraces in the old Italian style, with many plants and trees from the South. Perhaps because it was so early in the year the guides were not very vigilant and Drina was able to slip away into one of the beautiful, exotic corners where a fountain played, the sun touched the carved limbs of the statues, and oleanders and camellias encircled grass as short and smooth as green velvet.

She stood there, breathing in the sweet, hot air and gazing down at the waters of the lake where a scarlet boat and a turquoise blue one were just drifting out of sight.

To dance . . . to dance on Isola Bella in the lovely Italian sunshine!

There was not a soul about, though she could hear laughter in the distance. She kicked off her sandals and began to dance, remembering as she did so those other times that she had danced out of doors . . . long ago on that headland in the Lleyn Peninsula; on Romney Marsh under the vast sky; and in the Buckinghamshire woods.

Never, never had she thought to dance on an island in a lake, with just a glimpse of dazzlingly white peaks through the cypresses. Never, it seemed, had she been happy in quite this way. Never so conscious of the sun and the need to express happiness in movement.

But suddenly her graceful arabesque wavered and the dance was finished! There was someone amongst the trees!

Flushed and self-conscious, Drina turned to face Igor Dominick and, behind him, her grandmother.

"I just had to dance," she said hurriedly, thrusting her feet back into her sandals. "Are we leaving now?"

"But it was charming," said Signora Adamo. "So delightful a picture by the fountain!"

Igor Dominick patted his expensive little camera that he wore hanging round his neck by a thin strap. His dark face was much amused.

"A cover picture for a ballet magazine. What do you

say, Drina?"

"You didn't take it?" Drina gasped, not yet able to tell whether or not he was serious.

"I did. Didn't you hear the click? Well, it clicks very quietly, my camera."

"But you wouldn't – you couldn't –" Drina was appalled, and yet a little flattered, all the same.

"I might, if it's as good as I suppose. I shall call it 'Little Girl by a Fountain'." And he gave her such a wicked, teasing look that she said no more. It was odd how easily they were falling into friendship.

But, she told herself, it wouldn't last. It was just because he was lonely and they were on holiday. Back at the Dominick he would probably make friends of his own age – he was, after all, in the class above her – and that would be the end of that.

They had a delicious lunch in a garden by the lake and afterwards Drina and Igor explored the narrow, shadowy streets of old Stresa, which Drina greatly preferred to the broad modern promenade by the lake. And yet it was lovely to be by the water.

Afterwards they hired a red boat and Igor rowed placidly over the blue water while Drina trailed her fingers through its warmth. They did not talk much and she was glad. She wanted to savour every moment.

She was sun-flushed and dreamy as they sped back to Milan, and Igor and her grandmother did most of the talking, as they had done coming. They talked of Paris, of the ballet world, of art (Igor seemed to have a wide knowledge of painting), and of many other things besides. And when Drina and her grandmother were going up in the lift Signora Adamo remarked:

"A charming boy and so like his father and grandfather. I regretted that I had to take care and not let him know that I once knew them quite well."

"He is nice," Drina agreed. "And he seems to know an awful lot. But no one likes him at the Dominick."

"Because he did not want to leave Paris. But he will settle down and make friends. It is inevitable."

The day that had been so perfect ended with the performance of the new full-length ballet, *The Lonely Princess*. Received rather critically in London, it had had much advance publicity in the Italian papers and all seats had been sold a week before the Company arrived in Milan.

It was a far cry from the dress rehearsal at the Dominick Theatre to the brilliant and crowded opera house and Drina, looking back at her old self, could hardly believe that that dress rehearsal had taken place only a very few weeks ago. She felt older, more experienced, than the girl who had secretly dreaded the trip abroad.

But once the overture began the delightful music captured her and she sat with clasped hands, staring at the curtain, ready to lose herself in the ballet. And yet one part of her mind was conscious of all that would be going on behind the scenes. While the audience waited in anticipation, the dancers would still be warming up on the stage, ready to dart to their positions in the wings, the stage manager would be in the prompt corner waiting to give the signal for the curtain to rise, the electricians would be ready.

The curtains parted on the schoolroom scene and there was the fair-haired Princess bending over her books while the six governesses danced. There was the set with the big windows overlooking the woods and the distant village. Drina settled down to enjoyment, but forcing herself, as she sometimes did, to criticise.

"Say you had to write a critical piece for a newspaper?" she asked herself. "You mustn't always just sink into it. It's a bad habit."

She stayed critical until the curtain rose on the second act and then gave in to sheer pleasure. Besides, there was really so little to criticise. The *corps de ballet* was extraordinarily good that year – even the most stringent London ballet critics had said so repeatedly – the music, the sets and the costumes were somehow perfectly blended, and the choreography was at times nothing short of brilliant. The morris dance in the second scene of Act Two, for instance, and the Fool's virile solo. The *pas de quatre* for the May Queen's attendants was much more simple, but it was very charming. Drina leaned forward in her seat, watching each movement.

In the last act, as the tempo quickened and Court and villagers all danced at the wedding of the Prince and Princess, she allowed herself to be carried right away into that nameless rapture of movement, music and colour.

"It's been one of the nicest days I've ever known," she said dreamily as she and her grandmother drove through the brilliantly lighted streets. "I shall never forget it."

5

The Family
in Genoa

Thursday was Drina's last day in Milan and she did not realise with what great regret her Italian grandmother watched her moving about the flat. It had been a deep pleasure to have a young, attractive girl as a companion and Signora Adamo believed that, though they had not been close, they understood each other and that Drina would be glad to return to Milan.

In her own way Signora Adamo was nearly as undemonstrative as Mrs Chester, for though her family had originally come from the South she had absorbed much of the northern temperament, which did not so easily express thoughts and feelings. She had plenty of money, enjoyed a mildly social and artistic life in Milan and spent a good part of the year visiting her son and daughter or else friends in different parts of Italy. She had not been conscious of loneliness during the last few years, but, seeing Drina across the table or moving gracefully from room to room, she had certainly very forcibly remembered how different things might have been if she had won the child.

However, all this was in the past and, if Drina would now take it for granted that she had a second home in Italy, that would really do very well. So her grandmother told herself, but she wished that the visit might have been prolonged or that she had arranged to go to Genoa with her grandchild. But she was expecting an old friend to pay a visit in three days' time and had, in any case, decided long before that it would be better for Drina to get to know the Gardinos on her own. Antonia wanted an English friend and there was also Drina's own friend from the Dominick School, Emilia Riante. The young people would probably be out together a good deal. Yes, it was best . . . But she sighed as she settled down to write letters on that Thursday morning.

Drina went off cheerfully to meet Igor Dominick, since he had suggested a last drink together in Milan, but she was rather early, so she drifted along the pavement on the north side of the Piazza del Duomo, looking at the shop windows.

She was staring in fascination at the brilliantly coloured silks in one window when she saw out of the corner of her eye a familiar figure. Marianne Volonaise, in an extremely smart yellow suit, was only a foot or two away.

She recognised Drina at that moment and smiled in a friendly way. Drina could still be in awe of her – there were times when she looked remote and impressive and, after all, she held the fate of everyone at the Dominick School in her hands – but the day had gone when she thought herself more or less invisible in the august presence.

"Hullo, Drina!" said Marianne Volonaise, looking with appreciation at Drina's lightly tanned skin, shining hair and happy face. "You certainly look well! I suppose you got some of that tan at Stresa yesterday?"

Drina was startled. "Y – yes, I expect so. But –"

"I heard about young Igor going with you. It was very nice of you. The boy's lonely."

"I'm meeting him now," Drina said rather shyly. "Over by the statue. Only I was rather early."

"Good! And what do you think of the Dominick in Italy? The new ballet has several good write-ups this morning, far better than it got in London. Quite a pæan of praise."

"I thought it was wonderful," Drina said. "And I loved *Coppélia*, with the new set. La Scala is so – so impressive, too."

"It certainly is. We're lucky to be dancing there. Are you coming to see us again?"

"No, not in Milan. I'm going to Genoa tomorrow."

"Then you must come and see us there. And now I won't keep you from Igor." And she nodded and turned into the Galleria Vittorio Emanuele, walking with the singular grace that was the heritage of her dancing days.

Drina looked after her, jostled on the crowded pavement. Then she turned and crossed the road and found Igor Dominick the younger and Bettina Moore feeding the pigeons with crumbs out of a paper-bag. Bettina was laughing and looked very childish in her plain pink dress, and wearing very little make-up.

She did not seem to find it in the least beneath her to sit at a table drinking orangeade with a boy and girl so much younger than herself. In fact, she seemed to enjoy it and amused them by telling stories of her family in London. It seemed that she had four younger sisters and two brothers, so perhaps that partly explained her cheerful acceptance of younger company.

All the same, it did seem very strange to Drina to be with her and on such casually friendly terms, for she

had sat so often in the Dominick Theatre watching
Bettina dance and thinking how lucky she was to have
progressed so far in her career. Bettina as Little Clara,
so very childish in her long nightgown and with her
soft hair grown long and tied back with a blue ribbon;
ethereal and graceful in *Les Sylphides*; as a happy skater
in *Les Patineurs*; as a pawn in *Checkmate*.

The little waiter who had been so annoyed the day
Drina had no money now seemed almost a friend. He
greeted them as though he had known them for years.
And Milan itself seemed familiar and no longer alien,
though she still caught her breath sharply when she
looked up at the vast west front of the Cathedral, with
the pale pinnacles and the innumerable statues against
the blue and brilliantly white sky.

And tomorrow she would exchange Milan for
another Italian city; the high flat for a small villa close
to the Mediterranean.

"Shall I see you in Genoa, Drina?" Igor asked when
she stood up at last and said she must be going. And
Drina looked into his half-amused dark face and
grinned.

"If you like. Shall I write down the telephone
number?"

Igor nodded and Drina opened her shoulder-bag and
carefully wrote the Gardinos' number, already
memorised.

"I'll walk back with you," he said when he had put
the scrap of paper carefully away.

"And I'm going to write postcards to my family,"
Bettina said cheerfully, and waved them away.

As they neared the block of flats Igor asked with one
of his odd, amused looks, "And am I forgiven for
calling you a little girl?"

"Oh, yes," Drina said, laughing. "Of course."

"That's good. It wasn't really meant as an insult." And then he gave her a casual salute and turned away. "Until Genoa!"

"He's an odd boy," Drina thought. "But I do like him, in a cautious sort of way. Emilia will be quite surprised to find me friendly with him, after what I've told her about him. So remote and scornful-looking and speaking to almost no one. Anyway, I do believe he'll be different next term."

The next morning Drina was seen off at the station by her grandmother. Drina felt very sorry to say goodbye, though they had already arranged that she should come back whenever she wanted to do so, and it was lovely to think that when she went away from Italy she would know that she would certainly see it again, and perhaps other cities. Signora Adamo wanted to take her to Florence, Perugia and Rome.

In fact, the Drina who sat in a comfortable first-class seat, watching the outskirts of Milan give place to fields and small, palely coloured villages, seemed decidedly a different person from the uneasy and shy girl who had approached Victoria Station not a fortnight before. She looked back at her old self almost with shame, remembering how she had dreaded the Italian trip throughout the previous term.

"I must try never to be afraid of new experiences again. It's all been such fun, and some of it so wonderful. Getting to know Igor and Bettina. Seeing the Lakes and that beautiful garden where I danced on Isola Bella. And oh! La Scala! I shall never forget that."

Her grandmother had provided her with several magazines, but she was so busy with her thoughts that she scarcely glanced at them, and the train was drawing up in the Stazione Principe almost before she knew it. And there was Giulia Gardino on the platform, with a tall, curly-haired girl whom Drina immediately recognised from her grandmother's photographs. They greeted Drina warmly and the porter whisked the luggage away to the sunlit exit where the traffic whirled round the Piazza Acquaverde and Drina blinked up at tiers and tiers of cream and white and pink buildings on the steep hills above the city centre.

It was all a little dreamlike, as the arrival in Milan had been, and she did not say very much until they emerged on a wide boulevard, with smooth grass, brilliant flowerbeds and modern buildings, and then turned with one of the rapid sweeps of Italian taxi drivers and were very near the wide, pale blue Mediterranean.

The villa was small and green-washed, with shutters and balconies, and Drina's room looked through two pointed fir trees to a glimpse of the water. Antonia sat on the bed while she unpacked, and talked in an eager mixture of English and Italian, and Drina chattered back in the same two languages, but mainly in Italian which had grown surprisingly fluent during the time in Milan.

Antonia was fifteen and wore clothes of such simple elegance that she looked much older, but she was childishly pleased to meet her cousin from London and ready to listen by the hour to tales of the Dominick School and all Drina's friends. She went to a boarding-school outside Florence, but dismissed it as unutterably dull when compared to a dancing school, with a real ballet company next door.

They had lunch on the open veranda at the front of

the villa and the smell of pink roses just coming out kept drifting to Drina's nostrils. After the dust and noise of Milan it seemed altogether delightful and Drina felt a little more at home when she had had a long conversation with Emilia on the telephone. Aunt Giulia had said that Drina must ask her friend to visit them whenever she pleased, and Antonia seemed delighted at the prospect of meeting another future ballet dancer.

"But you must never tell her that Elizabeth Ivory was my mother," Drina begged, and her aunt and cousin looked at her in surprise.

"But why?" they both asked in Italian. Since Drina was reasonably at home in the language it was easier, they had decided by mutual consent, to give up the struggle to speak English.

"Because it's a secret. A very great secret." And Drina did her best to make them understand, which they seemed to do quite quickly.

That evening, as the early dusk settled over the garden and a pink light still touched the Mediterranean, Drina settled down to write to Jenny on the faraway Warwickshire farm. Her pen flew over the paper and page after page was hastily flicked to one side.

Dearest Jenny,

Well, I am here in Genoa (Genova, the Italians call it) and the Gardinos are awfully nice. I feel as though I've known them for a long time already. Uncle Giovanni – he's only my uncle by marriage, of course – is a surprisingly fair man, quite tall and with grey eyes. He laughs a lot and speaks better English than the other two. He has been to London several times, while Aunt Giulia and Antonia have never been and are very curious about it. Aunt Giulia is pretty and very, very smart, and Antonia wears lovely clothes, too. She makes me feel rather childish, for Granny never will let me have grown-up-looking clothes. She says that young people look their best in plain things. Actually Antonia's are quite plain, but they have real style. I think I shall ask Antonia to come and visit us in London quite soon; perhaps for a week or two in the summer, though of course it depends on what Granny and Grandfather and I are doing then. Granny did say something about going to the Edinburgh Festival this year, and then there's the farm and you.

It was exciting arriving in Genoa, though I couldn't take it all in. The Stazione Principe isn't so splendid as the station in Milan, but it's always exciting arriving in a new place. The Piazza Acquaverde outside the station seemed to be full of great buses, all swinging round a big statue of Christopher Columbus, and a lot of Genoa is on the hill behind, tiers and tiers of houses and churches. The taxi whirled us off down the Via Balbi, one of the famous streets with palaces in it and very narrow and dark in parts. And then down another famous street that Emilia used to talk about, even narrower and deeper, with more palaces. They are nearly all offices now. I couldn't see much, but there was a great horse-chestnut tree in full flower showing over a very high wall, so there must be gardens inside. There are strange long tunnels to take some of the traffic, called gallerie. Not in the least like the Galleria Vittorio Emanuele in Milan, which didn't take traffic at all.

The villa is a little way out of Genoa towards Nervi (that's the place where they have a wonderful open-air Festival in summer, and I remember the Dominick dancing there once), and it has a garden with a little fountain and lots of flowers. It seems strange to see roses coming out so early and lilac and laburnum, though Emilia did tell me, and it's been a very good spring, everyone says. They seem surprised to find it so warm and people are still going about in coats, while I was hot in my thin blouse.

After lunch we walked along by the Mediterranean, which isn't quite so blue as I expected, but it's lovely to be by the sea. Then we went to the Port, and that part is quite different; very old and peculiar and a trifle smelly, but awfully interesting with market stalls here and there and old women in black, laden with heavy baskets. I do find their faces interesting.

We cut up through some very narrow old streets, and some of the very poorest houses, with washing hanging outside, were once palaces belonging to the great Genoese families, Aunt Giulia told me. She showed me carvings over the doors and dates. The washing in Genoa is a thing that strikes you very much. It's hanging everywhere, all across the streets in the older parts of the city like strings of peculiar flags – you'd laugh if you could see some of the shirts and underwear all hung up in the public eye!

We went into the great palace where Uncle Giovanni works and it was most impressive, with a fountain playing in the courtyard and mosaic pavements and statues and wall paintings.

There are posters advertising the Dominick and oh! I am so glad that I'm in Italy at the same time. Antonia thinks it is romantic to be at a ballet school and knowing real dancers. You wouldn't agree with her, would you?

Give my love and a good stroke to Esmeralda and tell him that I'll see him in the summer. What a pity that he isn't a she with a lovely name like that! But then I really thought he was at first.

Oh, Jenny, I've never felt quite like me since I arrived in

Italy, but it's all wonderful and I'm very happy. I keep on feeling as though there's something more – something more exciting. And yet there can't be, except for seeing the Dominick again and exploring Genoa. Oh, and perhaps seeing Camogli, Santa Margherita and Rapallo. The Gardinos have a car and tomorrow and Sunday we're going out in it. Emilia is coming, too, tomorrow.

I think of you often and wonder what you would say about it all. When I started to write the sea had a pale pink light on it and I could just see the roses in the garden, but now it's quite dark, though there's going to be a moon.

Drina in Italy! I really can't quite believe it, or that in only just a week's time I shall be back in London, hearing dear old Big Ben and getting ready to go back to Red Lion Square.

Love from
Drina.

6

The unbelievable Thing

The sunny days flew by and Drina continued to be almost blissfully happy. On Saturday morning Emilia arrived at the villa very early and they set off eastwards in the car, through Nervi and on towards Camogli. To Emilia, of course, it was all familiar, but Drina was enchanted with each new vista. The colour-washed villas, the gardens filled with flowering trees and shrubs, the terraces of vines and the grey-green olive groves on the steep hills, the bright boats on the blue water, were like something out of a dream – not quite real.

And when they began to travel down the spiralling, steep road to Camogli she was tense with eagerness. She had heard so much from Emilia about the little Mediterranean fishing-port that she could hardly believe she was soon to see it for herself. They crept through the narrow old streets of the town and emerged by the harbour, where they parked the car and the two adult members of the party settled themselves at a café table and ordered wine.

Antonia and Emilia were so eager to show Drina everything that they would not wait for a drink, but hurried her off round the harbour, past the old men smoking their pipes and dreaming in the sun, the artists with their easels and busy paintbrushes, and the fishermen mending their nets. And Drina was wordless before the delight of the old peeling houses rising round the little harbour, the "skyscraper" houses of Camogli that she had heard and read about.

The smell of fish, boats and ropes seemed delightful and she laughed at the grubby, cheerful children playing everywhere.

Far out on a concrete breakwater they paused to look back at the picturesque scene and once again she longed to be able to paint. It must be so very satisfying to splash colour on to a big canvas. Almost more satisfying than learning to use one's body to interpret music and emotions.

"We could come again and go out in our friends' boat," Emilia said eagerly. "This morning, I know, they are in Genoa, but I could telephone and arrange it. Lucio is on holiday and he would take us round the promontory. Drina would love that."

"Oh, I should!" Drina cried.

From a high rock by the big white church they looked across the bay to where the Portofino promontory rose rocky and dark to the east, with here and there a tiny village apparently clinging to a precipice. Inside the church it was very quiet and seemed dim, in spite of the glittering lights. Old women were praying, so they tiptoed about, Drina strangely moved by the devout silence after the glare and life of the harbour.

Afterwards they walked along the little promenade, where there were many tiny cafés with tables and bright umbrellas on the pavement, but the "lido" was still not in use and no one was bathing in spite of the heat.

Antonia shook her head and said that no Italian would dream of bathing in April. The season was very far from having started.

She seemed to have taken to Emilia and kept on asking questions about the Dominick and their ballet training. Drina left Emilia to answer, for, most unusually, her mind was very far from dancing. She was content to be in the Mediterranean sunshine, hearing the musical sound of Italian voices and with her whole being satiated with colour.

They climbed the hill again and drove on to Rapallo, where they had lunch and then walked under some of the old stone arcades, looking at the shops. And Drina exclaimed in delight at the sight of a little painting of Camogli in a window. She insisted on going in and buying it, though it cost a lot of *lire*, and she said eagerly that it would hang over her bed in the Westminster flat, to remind her of Italy and sunshine on cold winter days.

Altogether it was a delightful day, and so was the next day, a Sunday, when they went westwards to Pegli and wandered and lazed in the sun. Drina was remembering dancing again, for the Dominick Company would be arriving in Genoa and rehearsing for the opening performance the next evening, when they were giving *Les Patineurs* and *Coppélia*, as on the first night in Milan.

On Monday Igor Dominick telephoned and Antonia and Drina met him outside the Opera House in the Piazza de Ferrari. Antonia had heard all about him and was obviously impressed by his good looks and easy grace. Igor, in his turn, appeared to admire Antonia, and they all three went up in the funicular to the heights above Genoa, where Drina was thrilled with the vast view – the whole of the city and the docks spread out below and the Riviera coast seen for miles in the clear light.

Emilia had been busy that morning, but had invited Antonia and Drina to lunch at the Riantes' flat in the Via XX Settembre. The flat had a stone balcony overlooking the great modern street and Drina could hardly be torn away from the interesting scenes below.

"How strange you must have found Chalk Green at first!" she cried, and Emilia laughed.

"Yes. I was like you and Rose and found the woods almost frightening. At night I lay awake missing the traffic. So you like our Via XX Settembre?"

"Yes, I do. It's very impressive. But I like the old, smelly parts best; the little squares and the tenements that used to be palaces, and the narrow streets."

"You're the first English visitor to do so, then!" said Emilia. "They mostly don't like Genoa at all, but they don't give it a chance. They just go on to Santa Margherita or Rapallo as quickly as they can."

"I love cities," Drina said. "Especially historic ones. I think Genoa is splendid and very beautiful in places. I love it already."

That evening Drina put on her scarlet dress, and Antonia an elegant white one, and with Signor and Signora Gardino went to see the Dominick Company at the Opera House. And, for nearly three hours, Drina once more forgot everything but the rapture of being in a theatre, watching ballet. Though she had seen the programme only a week before, the enchantment was the same and from the moment when the curtain rose on the first Act of *Coppélia* she was lost.

Antonia watched the first act in tense silence, her

body moving a little to the compelling music of the czardas, and at the end she turned to Drina.

"To think," she said in Italian, "that one day you'll do that. To think that you'll be dancing Swanilda and I shall watch you, perhaps!"

Drina sighed and then laughed, looking about her at the brightly dressed throng.

"Oh, Antonia! I may never dance Swanilda. But I *hope* I shall be in the *corps de ballet*. There's still no certainty at all that I shall even be taken into the Company."

"But of course. They are certain to accept you. Otherwise what is all this training for?"

"Some of the students at the Dominick School will teach," Drina said slowly. "But I should hate that. I want the theatre. Nothing else. And some of them will go into other companies, or find that they can't be dancers after all, and it might be me." For a moment fear clouded her whole mind and the future was dark. "I shan't even take my GCSEs for two years. Then, if I pass, and my dancing is good enough, I shall be a senior student of the School. So many things could happen –"

"You'll be a dancer," said Antonia, with utter conviction.

On Wednesday Emilia, Antonia and Drina set off from Genoa quite early in the morning, travelling by train to Camogli. The Gardinos had no objection to the girls going off on their own, especially as it had turned out that Signor Gardino knew the Lentardis, Emilia's Camogli friends. They were met at the station by Lucio Lentardi, a tall, suntanned young man, who seemed delighted to take them out in his boat.

The boat was painted blue and white and had a scarlet sail as well as an engine, and it was waiting by the harbour steps. They chugged their way out of the crowded harbour and then, out in the bay where there was a little breeze, the sail went up.

Emilia proved herself a skilful sailor, but Antonia and Drina were content to sit on the cushions, trailing their fingers in the water.

"It's perfect!" Drina breathed, as they sped under the high rocks of the promontory. "The water's so deep and clear and Camogli looks so beautiful, looking back."

They went out to sea in a wide arc and then swung back towards the southernmost point of the promontory where the narrow, deep harbour of San Fruttuoso cut into the rock. Lucio tied up the boat at the little landing-stage and insisted on showing Drina the famous Doria tombs in the deep vault of the rock.

San Fruttuoso seemed to Drina a strange place, so close under the promontory – a little dank and cold in spite of the warm sun shining on the water. She was glad when they decided to go on to Portofino and not to have coffee in the little restaurant. They were chugging slowly out of the harbour when another boat approached and Drina gave a startled cry.

"There's Igor! Look! In that motor-boat!"

Igor Dominick had seen her waving and seemed to give orders to the boatman at the controls. The motor-boat swung over and Lucio allowed his own boat to drift.

"Is this Igor Dominick Junior?" Emilia murmured, pushing her hair out of her eyes and staring with much interest.

Drina was standing up in the boat, a little surprised

by Igor's air of urgency. Gone was all his amusement and casualness and he was crying in what sounded like deep relief:

"Thank goodness! I *have* had a time!"

"You look for us, then?" Antonia asked in English.

"Indeed I have. First we telephoned the Riantes' flat, then we tried to get *you*," to Drina. "Marianne Volonaise was frantic when she learned that you had both gone out for the day. So then I offered to come and look for you and I hoped to catch you before you left Camogli. No one else could be spared – there is trouble on."

"But –" Drina and Emilia were gaping at him blankly, both standing up in the boat with their cotton skirts gently blowing about their bare legs.

"What is the matter?" Antonia asked calmly, while Lucio merely watched with polite interest.

"Matter?" For the first time Igor smiled in his usual way. "Lobster is the matter! Oh, yes, very much the matter!"

"*Tell* us!" Drina said frantically. "How *can* lobster be the matter? Oh, you are the most aggravating boy!"

Igor laughed and winked at her, but then spoke soberly, "Some members of the *corps de ballet* went last night to a restaurant by the Port, after the performance. All ate lobster that has disagreed with them. They're really ill. A doctor has been called and he says it is impossible for them to dance tonight. So Miss Volonaise and Miss Le Cain, the ballet mistress, want Drina and Emilia to dance in *The Lonely Princess*."

There was a perfectly blank silence, and then Drina moved. Her foot seemed to slip and she made a wild grab at the side of the boat. Her hand missed the gunwale and she went head-first into the deep green water.

For several moments she thought confusedly that she was going to the bottom and would never come up again; then she struggled to the surface and pushed the wet hair out of her eyes, staring up at their startled, dismayed faces.

"It can't be true! I don't believe it!" she gasped, treading water and ignoring the hands that reached towards her. "I just don't believe it!"

Life seemed to have had a dreamlike quality for a long time and now she was more sure than ever that she was not the Drina Adams who had left London a week or two before. To dance with the Dominick Company! To dance in Genoa when she was only fourteen and a half – it was such an unbelievable thing that she even forgot to tread water and went under again, to come up spluttering.

Lucio seized her firmly by one wet hand and Antonia helped to haul, since Emilia was still staring blankly. Drina arrived wetly in the boat and began to drip on to the cushions.

Igor, looking half-amused, half-dismayed, said, "Well, now what shall we do? You're as wet as a mermaid!"

The Italian boatman, who had never ceased an excited flood of speech since the moment when Drina went overboard, grew silent and shrugged. Patently the blue and white boat held more than one lunatic.

Drina squeezed out her skirt and tried to do the same to her heavy hair.

"Is it *really* true? You aren't teasing?"

Igor Dominick shrugged in a way that closely resembled the boatman's own expressive movement.

"It's quite true. Four of the lobster-eaters are the May

Queen's attendants. Two of the *corps de ballet* are to take their places, but no one else is small enough to wear the costumes. When everyone was in the most terrible state Miss Volonaise remembered the three members of the school. I also am to dance, as one of the village youths."

"Then we'll *have* to go!" Emilia exclaimed. "Oh, Drina, what shall we do about your wet clothes? You'll get cold –"

Lucio had been rooting in a locker and now produced two thick rugs which he wrapped round Drina. Emilia spoke rapidly to him in Italian and Igor paid off his own boatman and scrambled into the bigger boat. They swung out into the open sea and, with the breeze more or less behind them, headed rapidly for Camogli.

"I am sorry that the day is spoilt," Antonia said. "But to dance in Genoa with the Dominick Company! Oh, Drina, I *am* so glad that we have seats for tonight!"

Drina and Emilia exchanged glances that were not wholly delighted. Now that the first excitement had faded they were both thoroughly scared.

"The *pas de quatre*!" said Emilia, who had seen the ballet in London before her return to Italy. "It's quite simple really, but –"

"They speak of simplifying it still more," said Igor. "But Drina can't travel to Genoa in those wet clothes."

But Emilia had already planned it all in her own mind and the moment they reached the harbour, under many interested eyes, she whisked Drina from the boat and up the steps to the main street of the village. Fortunately the Lentardis lived in a house just above the little square, and there she explained matters to Signora Lentardi who was a very small woman, not much taller than Drina. Drina was put into a very hot bath and then provided with underclothes and a blue dress belonging to her hostess. It was only slightly too large and suited her quite well.

"Lucio will think us so rude!" Drina groaned as they hurried downstairs again.

"No, he won't," said Emilia. "He understands just how important it is."

Igor, who had been told to get Emilia and Drina back as quickly as possible, however much it cost, had hired a car and the three girls tumbled into the back seat.

"I shall have to fetch my practice clothes and shoes from the villa," Drina reminded them, rather breathlessly. "Oh, Antonia, I can't believe it's really happening!"

"Emilia must get hers also, but she lives quite close to the Opera House," Antonia remarked. She was definitely enjoying all the excitement.

After that Emilia and Drina sat in almost complete silence, while Igor, in the front seat, chatted to the driver in a mixture of French and very bad Italian.

As Nervi was left behind the hands of the two girls crept together and both were cold.

"It's just absolutely unbelievable!" said Drina.

7

The Lonely Princess

Drina leaped out of the car when it reached the villa and returned in only a minute or two with her practice clothes and ballet shoes. Her hair had dried by then, but it hung in untidy tangles and she kept on pushing them out of the way.

Antonia said, "Goodbye and good luck" and waved them away, and the car went on into the heart of Genoa. It stopped once again in the Via XX Settembre to allow Emilia to get her own practice things.

"We've not even had lunch!" she gasped as she returned to the back seat and thrust some biscuits into Drina's hand. Drina had not remembered to be hungry, but she was still eating the biscuits as they made their way in Igor's wake along a maze of passages to the wings, where several members of the Company exclaimed in relief at the sight of them.

The Company ballet mistress took one look at them and bustled them towards a large dressing-room where other female members of the Company were sitting about in various stages of undress.

"Thank goodness you're here! Miss Volonaise was sure that you'd come if you could be found. Drina Adams, isn't it? And Emilia Riante?" She took another look at Drina and nodded.

"Yes, I know you, of course. I saw *The Changeling*. Well, you'll probably manage pretty well. Change as quickly as you can."

"I feel sick!" wailed Emilia as she flung aside her clothes and began to thrust her limbs into her practice clothes.

"So do I. I think I *am* going to be sick!" Drina confessed miserably. "Oh, Emilia, I never thought it would be like this – the first time! I didn't even feel sure there *would* be a first time."

"Perhaps they'll throw us out after all," Emilia said gloomily. "I don't believe I can dance a step."

Drina ran a comb through her hair and tied it back with a ribbon. It was a relief when she saw Terza, looking comfortingly calm and cheerful.

"It is so nice to see you, Drina. Those poor things; ill with lobster!"

"You didn't eat it, then?" Drina asked.

"No. I had a sore toe and returned to my hotel. Now it seems as well that I did so."

Drina and Emilia went back to the wings and, though Drina still felt sick and tense, she was dimly conscious that it was good to be in a theatre again. The familiar smell of dust and wood and greasepaint was certainly a little comforting, but she was horribly afraid of the coming rehearsal.

Warming up, she felt a little better and so, apparently, did Emilia, for she grinned. Drina was glad that Emilia was there, too. She was not so close a friend as Rose or Jenny, or perhaps even as Ilonka had grown, but they had shared a room for two and a half terms and also many experiences.

For an hour Drina, Emilia and two of the youngest

and smallest members of the *corps de ballet* practised the slightly simplified version of the *pas de quatre* in the second act and gradually Drina and Emilia grew more confident. The ballet mistress, of whom at first they were terribly in awe, was kind and nothing but helpful, and Marianne Volonaise made occasional comments. There was no sign of Mr Dominick and during a brief pause his son remarked to Drina that he had gone back to England, leaving the Company's affairs in the hands of their general manager.

"Miss Volonaise is returning to London on Saturday, too," he explained. "And I am accompanying her. School, of course, starts on Tuesday morning."

And Drina, who was travelling on Friday evening with some friends of the Gardinos, thought fleetingly that she might have travelled with them.

But there was little time for thinking. A full rehearsal of both scenes in the second act followed almost at once, and then Act Three, the wedding scene at the Palace. Drina, Emilia and the other two attendants were there, of course, but they were only to join in one ensemble at the very end. Otherwise the act was slightly altered to allow them simply to attend the Princess and not to dance.

After that, weak with hunger and strain, Drina and Emilia were borne off by the wardrobe mistress to try on the costumes. Emilia, who was two inches taller than Drina, was quite easy to fit, but Drina was so slight and small that even the smallest costumes were inclined to slip off her shoulders and they would have to be altered to fit her.

It was half past five before Drina had a chance to telephone to the villa to say that she was going home with Emilia for a meal. She had to tell Antonia exactly what had happened and to be assured that she would get an extra special round of applause from the Gardino family.

"Father is coming in your place," Antonia told her. "He isn't very interested in ballet, but says he must see you dance."

"Oh dear!" Drina sighed. "I hope it will be all right. I don't seem to have any stomach at all!"

"That's because you're hungry. Think of your mother. You couldn't possibly dance badly."

But the fact that she had had a very great ballerina for a mother was no comfort to Drina as she and Emilia walked in the early evening sunlight down the Via XX Settembre. She still wore Signora Lentardi's clothes and that fact helped to make her feel unlike herself.

Bianca and Signora Riante received the two pale, tired girls with many exclamations of excitement and interest, but Emilia's mother soon realised that they were almost too exhausted to speak and she made them sit down and drink some soup before they said another word. The good soup brought life back into their bodies and made them realise that they were, in fact, half-dead with hunger. And after that they ate veal and salad with fair appetites.

"To think!" cried Emilia, "I shall be back at Chalk Green on Wednesday!"

"I wish we could have travelled together," Drina remarked. "But the Dominick starts on Tuesday morning and I never thought of it."

"I'm flying back on Wednesday morning," Emilia told her. "Bianca as well, of course. We shall be met at the airport and be at Chalk Green by late afternoon."

"And you will be able to say that you danced with the Dominick Company," remarked Bianca, still much awed. Her English was fairly good after a term at the Buckinghamshire boarding-school and she was very pretty, though rather shy.

At that Drina and Emilia gave concerted groans and went out on to the stone balcony to look down at Via XX Settembre.

The stone balustrade was still warm after the heat of the day, but the air had grown chilly and Drina was glad of the jacket she had borrowed from Emilia. As she gazed down at the busy Genoese street, with its shining cars and its crowds of hurrying people, she wished with all her heart that the evening was over.

She had longed to know that she would dance with the Dominick Company, but the chance seemed to have come too soon and too abruptly. It was, in fact, quite impossible to believe in the reality – that in less than an hour they must go back to the theatre.

"I wonder what Granny would say if she knew?" Drina mused, and was suddenly visited by a nostalgic picture of her grandmother, so restrained and calm. She would probably be preparing the evening meal at that very minute and perhaps pausing to look out at the view from the living-room window, a sideways glimpse of the trees in Victoria Tower Gardens and a corner of the Houses of Parliament.

Drina leaned there on the balustrade, glad that Emilia did not seem to want to talk, thinking that life was very strange and surprising.

Fright continued to be Drina's main emotion as time passed and the moment for going on stage drew nearer. And yet there was also a deep and wild excitement once she was made up and wearing the charming white dress and flowery head-dress for the second act of Scene Two. The dress for the last act, the wedding scene, was palest pink, a mass of short, foamy skirts.

It was rather hot in the dressing-room and she still felt rather sick, but it was comforting to feel that everyone was friendly and encouraging. Bettina, like Terza, had gone to bed instead of going on to the restaurant by the Port, and she was very nice to both the shivering members of the Dominick School.

"You'll be all right once you get on stage," she assured them, and Emilia said wretchedly:

"I suppose so. But my stomach feels terrible."

They watched the first scene of Act Two from the wings and happiness gradually began to master Drina's fright and nausea. After all, it was simply wonderful to think of dancing with the Dominick Company in Italy! The smell of the theatre, the lovely music, the presence of the huge and seemingly tense audience, began to get into her blood.

They warmed up in a corner while the stage hands changed the scene, and then it was almost time for the curtain to rise on the village green. The morris men teased the two latest additions to the Company and Emilia and Drina grinned and dodged out of the way of Jack-in-the-Green and his cumbersome cage.

Even Catherine Colby put her hands on their bony shoulders and said, "It's really very sporting of you at such short notice. Good luck, girls!"

"We *can't* disgrace ourselves!" Drina said. "And think how marvellously exciting it will be to look back on!"

Emilia nodded, and then the music began, and a minute or two later the curtain rose on the maypole dance and the village people preparing for the crowning ceremony, only to find that they had no Queen. The arrival of the Princess was very opportune and they crowded round her, urging her to agree to being their May Queen.

The lights, the music, the whole atmosphere of the ballet, suddenly caught Drina up into something of the sharp enchantment that she often felt when watching from the front of the circle. Only this was different. This was real. She really was there amongst the dancers, excited and eager, ready to dance before the flower-decked throne.

When the time came for the *pas de quatre* she danced with assurance and grace; no longer in the least afraid, but only enjoying being on a stage again, before an audience. It seemed a very long time since that afternoon in December when she had danced the name part in *The Changeling* and gone in front of the curtain afterwards to curtsy.

The scene ended with everyone dancing round the King and Queen and the Prince and Princess and when the curtain came swiftly down Emilia cried in a startled voice, "But it was *fun*! Oh, Drina, didn't you like it?"

And Drina could only nod, for now that the second act was over she found that her throat was dry and she could hardly swallow.

They tore along the passages to their dressing-room and took off the white dresses with rather clumsy fingers. The pink dress was still a trifle too large for Drina and it had to be sewn up while she tried not to wriggle. The ballet mistress looked in while the sewing was in progress and smiled very kindly.

"Well done, Drina and Emilia!" she said. "The *pas de quatre* was charming."

It seemed miraculous that they were being praised by

anyone so august and when Marianne Volonaise herself said nearly the same thing it seemed almost too much.

Drina consciously enjoyed every moment of the third act. They had not much to do and it was very thrilling to watch the *divertissement* from so near at hand. She was part of the ballet, part of the Company, just for one night.

"Soon it will be over," Drina thought, as the music moved on towards the finale. "Soon the curtain will come down and the lights will go out and everyone will go home."

She was so warmly filled with a sharp and almost unbelievable happiness that one observant reporter in the audience noticed her airy rapture and wrote the next day:

The very English three-act ballet, *The Lonely Princess*, was, on the whole, a delight as well as a curiosity for an Italian audience. The music was tuneful and lent itself perfectly to the ballet movements and the dancing of the ballerina, Miss Catherine Colby, was beyond praise. Mr Peter Bernoise as the Woodcutter-Prince also deserves great praise. His elevation is remarkable and he is a most polished and elegant dancer. I particularly enjoyed the simple *pas de quatre* by four young dancers, and one of these, at the end of the last act of the ballet, seemed lighter than air. One felt her pleasure in the dance most acutely, this little black-haired girl who looked so very young to be a member of this great Company.

But that was the next morning, to be read out excitedly by Antonia and then translated from the Italian by Drina herself.

That night, as the curtain came down for the last

time, Drina and Emilia took hands and went very slowly back to the dressing-room.

"I shall never forget it," said Drina. "Not any of it. What a strange day it's been and so very long! It seems like a year since we went out in the boat and Igor came to tell us –"

At that moment Igor himself came up to them, looking almost unrecognisable in the heavy make-up and the slim-fitting costume of a village youth.

"Well? It was amusing, didn't you think?"

They nodded, and Drina asked, "Was it your first time, too? With the Company – any company?"

"I walked on once or twice in Paris, but that's all. The lobster gave us all a chance."

"I wonder what he'll be like next term?" Drina mused as they undressed and began to scramble into their ordinary clothes, suddenly conscious that they were very tired. "He is so much nicer than anyone thought."

Then the three Gardinos came backstage to fetch her home and they drove away down the brilliantly lit Via XX Settembre.

The strange and unforgettable day was almost over.

8

Home again

"You will come back," said Antonia, on the platform of the Stazione Principe at nearly eight o'clock on Friday night. It was a statement, not a question, and Drina nodded.

"I hope so. Oh, I hope so, Antonia! I've loved Italy."

"And I shall come to London."

Drina looked up into the pretty face of her Italian cousin and nodded again.

"Of course you will, and I'll show you everything. The parks and the Tower and Westminster Abbey. And, of course, Covent Garden and the Dominick Theatre."

"And I shall perhaps see you dance again."

But at that Drina shook her head.

"Not for years and years, probably. That once was just a – a sort of miracle."

It was almost dark and she remembered suddenly that the Dominick Company would be dancing at that very moment. Up above the station the tiers of houses and churches were darkly silhouetted against the fading light of the sunset, and it seemed strange to think that by the next evening she would be back in London, with the Italian holiday just a wonderful memory.

The train, with its sleeping-cars, had come from Rome and already seemed fairly full. But Drina had a sleeper to herself and she soon settled down on the top berth. She was sure that she would not sleep, for her mind was so full of memories of her last day, of all the days since she had come to Italy. But she slept all night long, waking only briefly to peer out at Turin.

In Paris the sky was grey and the wind was cold and she put on her coat, which she had scarcely needed at all in Italy, and walked about the station alone, since her travelling companions did not want to leave the train in spite of the long wait.

Drina had some French francs, provided originally for meals on the French trains, and she used them up by buying postcards of Sacré Coeur, Notre Dame and the River Seine from the air. She had a fruit drink at the station restaurant and then bought a few packets of sweets to add to her presents. For her grandmother she was taking a pink and grey silk scarf, a leather wallet for her grandfather and a little scarlet handbag for Jenny. For Rose there was a tiny Italian doll for a mascot, and an emerald green and gold scarf for Ilonka.

It was so strange to be so briefly in Paris and Drina wondered if she would ever get to know the city. It seemed that she probably would one day.

The Channel was choppy, but Drina walked the deck in the cold wind until the white cliffs of Dover were in sight; then she went below for a hot drink before landing. The two Italian ladies with whom she was travelling had not enjoyed the journey and were only looking forward to reaching their London hotel. But they were kind to Drina and admired her for her "fortitude" in walking the cold deck and not being even remotely boat- or train-sick.

It was almost May and cherry-blossom had given place to apple and pear and plum blossom, some of it already falling in the strong wind. It was a cloudy evening and rain was beginning to fall as the long boat train slid into Victoria.

Drina parted with her companions on the platform, saying that she would be quite all right and thanking them politely for seeing her back to England. In her heart she felt that she would have managed perfectly well. Travel seemed extremely easy and she had undoubtedly gained in confidence.

At the barrier were Mr and Mrs Chester and Rose, the latter looking pale and cold but smiling delightedly.

Mrs Chester greeted Drina with a cool little kiss and remarked that she really looked extremely well and surprisingly sunburnt. Mr Chester, slightly more demonstrative, gave her a brief warm hug and Rose chattered eagerly as they went towards the car.

"Your grandmother said I could come home with you for supper and your grandfather is going to take me home later. Isn't it nice of him? Oh, Drina, you do look wonderful! Did you really enjoy it?"

"Every moment!" Drina assured her, but she determined to keep the most exciting news until later. Rose would be staggered and envious to hear that she had danced with the Dominick Company.

Rose certainly looked anything but "wonderful". She said that the holiday had seemed long and that she was looking forward to getting back to Chalk Green and the strong air of the hills.

They drove away along Victoria Street and Drina looked out at the familiar London scene with eyes that still remembered so well the contrasts of Genoa.

The flat seemed very warm and cosy after the chilly, damp evening and there was a gala supper, with some of Drina's favourite dishes.

"Only don't eat too much," Mrs Chester said. "If you do you won't sleep a wink." But Drina tackled everything with appetite. It was good to be home again and enjoying her grandmother's cooking, even though she had liked Italian food so much.

Over the meal she began to tell them about her experiences, and Rose's eyes grew wider and wider at the story of the lobster and several members of the *corps de ballet* not able to dance. Mrs Chester, on the other hand, listened to the story in rather grim silence. She had long ago realised that Drina must be allowed to dance, with the almost certain knowledge that she would make it her profession in the years to come, but she would have preferred her not to have tasted the obviously heady pleasure of dancing in a foreign country when only fourteen.

"I suppose you *had* to help them out," she said unwillingly, at the end. "But don't let it give you ideas, Drina dear. After all, you may not be taken into the Company when the time comes."

Drina, who knew that very well without being reminded, gave a small shudder which Rose eyed with sympathy.

"Granny, of course that's true, but I can't face it. And it was so wonderfully exciting to dance in Genoa, though both Emilia and I felt sick until almost the last minute."

"I wish you wouldn't get so worked up about things," said Mrs Chester. "But I must say you look extremely well and not tired. I expected you to be half-dead after the journey. All the same, you mustn't go to bed too late. By the way, there are some letters for you. One from Jenny and one that looks very like a business letter. You'd better open it."

The letter, which was typed, startled Drina very much. It was from the well-known producer, Calum Campbell, the man who had produced the play, *Argument in Paris*, in which Drina had once played the part of the young dancer, Francoise. He explained that he was planning to put on a short season of Barrie's plays in the summer. *The Admirable Crichton*, *What Every Woman Knows* and *Mary Rose* had already been cast, but there were still some parts to be filled in *Dear Brutus*. Would Drina like to be auditioned for the part of Margaret? He thought that she would probably be chosen. He had actually consulted Mr Dominick and Miss Volonaise before they left for Italy and neither had any objection. The play would only run for a fortnight at the Queen Elizabeth Theatre and need not interrupt her dancing too much.

Drina read the letter aloud, her cheeks burning and her heart thumping.

"Well, what shall you do about it?" her grandfather asked. Mrs Chester was silent with deep dismay. She had no more wish for Drina to be an actress rather than a dancer and it would mean, if she got the part, all the trouble and anxiety of arranging for someone to accompany her to rehearsals and performances, and probably a good deal of unwelcome publicity. She had not forgotten the time when the flat seemed full of half-read newspapers, when the critics were writing about *Argument in Paris*.

"Oh, Drina, how exciting!" Rose cried.

Drina's face was very grave, after the first shock of pleasure and excitement.

"I love *Dear Brutus*. In some ways it's my favourite play. And to act Margaret – just that one long scene in the wood! But I want to dance, not act, and I think I ought to work especially hard this term."

"Well, think about it," said her grandmother. "I shan't try to influence you, but it does seem better that you should stick to your dancing."

Rose left with Mr Chester half an hour later and Drina soberly prepared for bed. Italy had already receded and she was half-lost in thoughts of *Dear Brutus*. She had bought a secondhand copy of Barrie's plays and she read the scene in which Margaret appeared before falling asleep. It might be wonderful, and yet –

On Saturday morning Ilonka arrived at the flat. Her cheeks were bright red and her eyes were shining. She, at least, looked as though the holidays had agreed with her. She hurled herself on Drina in a way that Mrs Chester thought far too emotional and foreign, but even she was filled with warm sympathy and pleasure when she heard Ilonka's wonderful news. They had had word that Mr Lorencz had arrived safely in Vienna and he was flying to England that very day.

Ilonka cried a little with pure happiness as she told them.

"We can't believe – none of us can believe. We thought we might never see him again."

"Oh, Ilonka, I'm so very glad!" Drina gasped and a small cloud of horror rolled off her mind. Ever since hearing Ilonka's story she had hated to remember the father left behind, perhaps still in prison and never to be free and happy with his family.

"So now everything is perfect," Ilonka said, flicking a

little pink handkerchief across her eyes. "Terza is happy, and Mother is happy, and I shall go on learning to be a good dancer."

That afternoon Rose and Drina walked in St James's Park and the sun was bright, reflecting back from the still waters of the lake.

Drina told about Ilonka's good news and Rose agreed that it was simply wonderful and that it was a pity Terza couldn't add another chapter to *Diary of a Dancer*. Then they talked about the coming term, both at Chalk Green and the Dominick, but suddenly Rose stopped to say:

"It won't be an ordinary term for you, though. All the exciting things happen to you, Drina. I'm sure you'll get that part –"

Drina shook her head.

"Do you know, Rose, I've been thinking very hard. It's tempting, because I do love Margaret and I think I could do it. I'd *love* to do it. But I don't mean to be an actress and I mustn't take any time at all off from my dancing. I'm going to write to Mr Campbell tonight and thank him, but say that I shan't be going to the audition."

Rose stared. Drina was always surprising her by her unusual decisions.

"Are you sure it isn't because your grandmother doesn't approve?"

"Quite sure. I hate hurting or annoying Granny, but if I wanted to do it I should. I've got to make my own life; I've always known that, and Granny does, too, really. No, I mean it about dancing. It wouldn't only be for a fortnight; there'd be rehearsals and all sorts of distractions. No, I'll stick to the Dominick and work like anything next term. Dancing in Italy showed me more clearly than ever that being in the Company is the only thing I want."

They walked on in silence for some time while the birds sang in the brilliantly green trees and children shouted and laughed, throwing bread to the water-fowl and watching them fight and dive.

"I suppose it's right," said Rose at last and Drina nodded.

"I think it is. I'm sure it is, really. Anyway, I've made up my mind."